PRAISE FOR TAMMY L. GRACE

"I had planned on an early night but couldn't put this book down until I finished it around 3am. Like her other books, this one features fascinating characters with a plot that mimics real life in the best way. My recommendation: it's time to read every book Tammy L Grace has written."
— *Carolyn, review of Beach Haven*

"*A Season of Hope* is a perfect holiday read! Warm wonderful and gentle tale reflecting small town romance at its best."
— *Jeanie, review of A Season for Hope: A Christmas Novella*

"This book is a clean, simple romance with a background story very similar to the works of Debbie Macomber. If you like Macomber's books you will like this one. The main character, Hope and her son Jake are on a road trip when their car breaks down, thus starts the story. A holiday tale filled with dogs, holiday fun, and the joy of giving will warm your heart.

— Avid Mystery Reader, review of A Season for Hope: A Christmas Novella

"This book was just as enchanting as the others. Hardships with the love of a special group of friends. I recommend the series as a must read. I loved every exciting moment. A new author for me. She's fabulous."
—Maggie!, review of Pieces of Home: A Hometown Harbor Novel (Book 4)

"Tammy is an amazing author, she reminds me of Debbie Macomber… Delightful, heartwarming...just down to earth."
— Plee, review of A Promise of Home: A Hometown Harbor Novel (Book 3)

"This was an entertaining and relaxing novel. Tammy Grace has a simple yet compelling way of drawing the reader into the lives of her characters. It was a pleasure to read a story that didn't rely on theatrical tricks, unrealistic events or steamy sex scenes to fill up the pages. Her characters and plot were strong enough to hold the reader's interest."
—MrsQ125, review of Finding Home: A Hometown Harbor Novel (Book 1)

"This is a beautifully written story of loss, grief, forgiveness and healing. I believe anyone could relate to the situations and feelings represented here. This is a read that will stay with you long after you've completed the book."
—Cassidy Hop, review of Finally Home: A Hometown Harbor Novel (Book 5)

"Killer Music is a clever and well-crafted whodunit. The vivid and colorful characters shine as the author gradually reveals their hidden secrets—an absorbing page-turning read."

— Jason Deas, bestselling author of Pushed and Birdsongs

"I could not put this book down! It was so well written & a suspenseful read! This is definitely a 5-star story! I'm hoping there will be a sequel!"

—Colleen, review of Killer Music

"This is the best book yet by this author. The plot was well crafted with an unanticipated ending. I like to try to leap ahead and see if I can accurately guess the outcome. I was able to predict some of the plot but not the actual details which made reading the last several chapters quite engrossing."

—0001PW, review of Deadly Connection

COME HOME FOR CHRISTMAS

COME HOME FOR CHRISTMAS

HOMETOWN HARBOR SERIES BOOK 9

TAMMY L. GRACE

LONE MOUNTAIN PRESS

COME HOME FOR CHRISTMAS
A novel by
Tammy L. Grace

www.tammylgrace.com
Facebook: https://www.facebook.com/tammylgrace.books
X(Twitter): @TammyLGrace

Published in the United States by Lone Mountain Press, Nevada

ISBN 978-1-945591-76-1 (paperback)
ISBN 978-1-945591-74-7 (eBook)
FIRST EDITION
Cover by Elizabeth Mackey Graphic Design
Printed in the United States of America

ALSO BY TAMMY L. GRACE

COOPER HARRINGTON DETECTIVE NOVELS

Killer Music

Deadly Connection

Dead Wrong

Cold Killer

Deadly Deception

HOMETOWN HARBOR SERIES

Hometown Harbor: The Beginning (Prequel Novella)

Finding Home

Home Blooms

A Promise of Home

Pieces of Home

Finally Home

Forever Home

Follow Me Home

Long Way Home

CHRISTMAS STORIES

A Season for Hope: Christmas in Silver Falls Book 1

The Magic of the Season: Christmas in Silver Falls Book 2

Christmas in Snow Valley: A Hometown Christmas Book 1

One Unforgettable Christmas: A Hometown Christmas Book 2

Christmas Wishes: Souls Sisters at Cedar Mountain Lodge

Christmas Surprises: Soul Sisters at Cedar Mountain Lodge

GLASS BEACH COTTAGE SERIES

Beach Haven

Moonlight Beach

Beach Dreams

WRITING AS CASEY WILSON

A Dog's Hope

A Dog's Chance

WISHING TREE SERIES

The Wishing Tree

Wish Again

Overdue Wishes

One More Wish

SISTERS OF THE HEART SERIES

Greetings from Lavender Valley

Pathway to Lavender Valley

Sanctuary at Lavender Valley

Blossoms at Lavender Valley

Comfort in Lavender Valley

Reunion in Lavender Valley

Remember to subscribe to Tammy's exclusive group of readers for your gift, only available to readers on her mailing list. **Sign up at www.tammylgrace.com. Follow this link to subscribe at https:// wp.me/P9umIy-e** and you'll receive the exclusive interview she did with all the canine characters in her Hometown Harbor Series.

Follow Tammy on Facebook by liking her page. You may also follow Tammy on book retailers or at BookBub by clicking on the follow button.

"At Christmas, all roads lead home." —Marjorie Holmes

CHAPTER ONE

R elieved that office hours were over until the new term started after winter break, Professor Noelle Davis walked the last student out of her office and closed the door. As she slipped into her desk chair, a soft knock came from the other side of her office door.

Kim, her assistant, came through the door with a file and a tentative smile. "Here's all the information from the school district in Friday Harbor. I booked your ride to the airport, printed your boarding pass, and have you booked on the ferry shuttle. There's also a copy of your reservation at the B&B."

"Thanks, Kim." She took the heavy plastic file folder and slipped it into her leather purse that was more like a tote bag.

Kim consulted her notepad. "Professor Abrams is all set to proctor the final exam for you next week, and I'll make sure the TA gets the grades submitted."

Noelle smiled at Kim and plucked a gift bag from the side table. "Sounds good. I appreciate all your help and hope you have a wonderful Christmas."

As she took the bag, Kim grinned. "Thanks so much, Professor Davis. I know you'll be working on the audit, but I hope you enjoy your time on the island. I've never been there but looking at the photos online, it looks lovely."

Noelle nodded. "I'll see you after the break, Kim. I'm heading home to finish packing."

Kim left her with a wave and shut the door behind her.

Noelle sighed and checked her email one more time, with the hope she might have a message from her daughter Courtney. Her shoulders sagged as she scanned the messages. Nothing from Courtney.

She turned on her out of office automated reply and shut down her computer. As she reached for her laptop bag, her eyes rested on the framed photo she cherished. It was old, taken at Christmas years ago, with her mom holding Courtney, both decked out in holiday dresses, sitting in front of the tree.

This would be the first Christmas without her mom, and Courtney, in her last year of college, was spending the break with her fiancé and his family, who was treating her to a ski vacation in Vermont.

Noelle only learned about the fiancé at Thanksgiving when Courtney surprised her with the news. Thank goodness, they weren't planning a wedding anytime soon, but Noelle understood her little girl wasn't coming home. She was making her own way and forging her own path. It's what mothers wanted, but it didn't make it hurt any less.

Noelle loved Christmas, but this year, it was shaping up to be a horrible holiday.

Her life wasn't what she imagined. Noelle's husband Tom died years ago, when Courtney was very young. She missed him always, but the holidays were especially hard.

More so this year.

She hadn't had time to build a relationship with anyone new, and the regrets of that weighed heavily on her all these years later. She'd given up on the idea of being married again but missed the companionship. Her faithful dog passed away this summer, so she didn't even have the comfort of her furry friend. The last months had been some of the saddest she'd experienced.

Her house was too quiet and if she was honest, her life was a lonely one.

As she blinked back tears, she lugged the laptop bag and slipped her purse on her arm. With her mother gone and Courtney three thousand miles away, she looked forward to spending the holiday away from home on San Juan Island.

It didn't take her long to drive from Walla Walla University to her house in a quiet neighborhood less than a mile away. She deposited her laptop bag by the front door and stepped into the quiet space.

She didn't even have a tree up this year. Her heart wasn't in it.

As was her routine, Noelle changed out of her work clothes and into comfy pajamas. Her suitcase was open on her bed, and she gazed over the checklist she used for travel and added in the remaining items.

The bright sticky note reminded her to cancel her hair appointment. She hated to do that as her pesky gray roots were showing in her dark-brown hair, and the magic of copper highlights her hairdresser added were fading. With great reluctance, she texted her and asked to reschedule for January.

She picked up the folder that was next to the suitcase and opened it.

Inside was the letter that prompted her to take the audit

project on San Juan Island. She'd read the letter dozens of times but couldn't resist another look.

She carried it with her to the kitchen where she stared at the two mugs on the counter. She and her mom always started their morning with tea and a visit. She couldn't bring herself to put her mom's mug away forever. It was a plain beige one lettered with "MOM" above a simple pink heart. She reached out and ran her finger over the rim. What she wouldn't give for another chance to visit over a cup of tea. There was never enough time.

Noelle poured a glass of wine and curled into the corner of the couch.

Her mother's perfect handwriting stared back at her from the pages of the letter. As she reread it, sadness settled over her. She loved her parents so much and, after her dad died, had spent most of her spare time with her mom. Losing her was like losing her best friend.

Her eyes blurred as she read the part about being adopted. As much as Noelle tried to understand her mother's words, she wished she would have uttered them long ago. She hated reading it in a letter and being unable to ask questions.

The revelation from her mother was the other reason she was happy to make the trek to San Juan Island. The sentence her mother wrote was burned into her mind. *You were left at the door of the fire station in Friday Harbor on December 22.*

Turns out whoever left Noelle at the door fifty years ago only included a short note that said the baby was born on December 21, and she couldn't take care of her and was sorry but wanted her to have a good life.

The letter from her mom explained her parents had no idea who her birth mother was, and they were the ones who chose to name her Noelle, in honor of her being born near Christmas.

As she gently refolded the papers, including the fifty-year-old note from her birth mother, and tucked them back in the envelope, tears leaked from her eyes.

She hoped she wasn't setting herself up for a huge disappointment, but when the email came through the university about the audit project at the school district, she took it as a sign. The university partnered with local governments to offer pre-audits free of charge and approved the request from the school district. Projects like theirs went out to staff, and interested professors could apply to conduct them. Her seniority and expertise in governmental accounting made her a shoe-in.

The university was giving her three days off before the holiday break to conduct the audit and paying for her flights and room for those days. She was booked to stay through the holidays and return the first week of January. Of course, she had to pay for the extra lodging, but it was worth it.

Along with not wanting to spend Christmas at home alone, Noelle was determined to find out more about her birth parents and the place she'd been left when she was born.

CHAPTER TWO

As Noelle trudged to the curb Saturday morning, where her rideshare driver waited, she yawned. It was four o'clock in the morning and pitch dark. She hadn't slept well and was already bracing for the stress of travel.

Walla Walla had a very small airport and limited flights. She opted for the early morning one since she had to take a ferry and didn't want to end up arriving late in the evening.

As her eyes burned from lack of sleep, Noelle doubted her flight choice.

Within fifteen minutes, she was at the terminal, which wasn't busy. She checked in and got to the gate with plenty of time to spare.

She sent Courtney a text to let her know she was on her way to the island. She chose not to tell Courtney about her personal reason for making the trip to San Juan Island and only told her there was an audit to do, and she was extending her time there to spend the holidays.

At this point, Noelle wasn't sure Courtney cared all that much. She was wrapped up in her own life and the promise of a ski vacation. Noelle chalked up her grumpiness to a lack of sleep and tried to be happy for Courtney. It was an exciting time for her daughter.

She wanted to share in that happiness but couldn't help but contemplate her future life. One that would no doubt be very lonely. Unless she moved across the country to be closer to her daughter and her new husband. The thought of retirement loomed in the back of her mind.

Noelle shook her head when she considered moving closer to Courtney. She didn't want to be one of those mothers.

After a few minutes, Noelle's phone chimed, and she smiled at the quick reply from Courtney wishing her a safe flight.

Minutes later, she was seated on the small plane, hoping she might sleep, but the loud hum of the propellers on the plane made it impossible.

The flight was a little over an hour and once she collected her bag, she checked the time and found the correct door she would need to use to catch the shuttle to the ferry. She had over an hour and opted to sit and enjoy a latte.

As she ordered, she perused the case of pastries and other snacks. She was starving but a bit queasy and not a great traveler. She opted to forgo food and stick with a chai tea latte.

Unlike Walla Walla, the Seattle airport was bustling and decked out for the holidays. After people watching, she was even happier to live in the small town close to where she worked.

She chuckled as she sipped the last of the latte. At least she hadn't been left at a fire station in a big city like Seattle. From what the school district staff told her, she could walk anywhere she needed to get to in Friday Harbor. Her B&B

was close to the harbor, and the school district arranged for someone to pick her up on Monday morning and drive her the three blocks to their office.

If she needed a car, there was a rental place connected to the local auto repair shop, but the woman on the phone assured her that she wouldn't need to worry.

The idea of a small-town Christmas appealed to her, but it wasn't at the top of her mind. Finding out who she really was—that was what she wanted for Christmas this year.

She tossed the empty cup and made her way to the exit where she walked to the designated section and scanned the shuttle area for the name of the one she needed. People and cars buzzed all around her as panic rose in her throat when she didn't see the shuttle.

Confident in the name she committed to memory, she kept looking and finally spied it tucked between two others. She hurried to the door, and the older gentleman at the wheel welcomed her with a smile and stowed her bag in the luggage area.

Relieved, she took her seat and checked her watch. She hoped to make the noon sailing but tamped down the nervous feeling she had about missing it by checking the schedule she'd texted herself. There were four more sailings after that one, so she needn't worry.

The older she got, the less she enjoyed traveling, especially alone.

As the driver announced their departure and let his passengers know it would take over two hours to get to the ferry dock, he steered the shuttle van away from the curb. Noelle relaxed and settled her head against the cushioned seat. It was quiet, with very few people on the shuttle, and she opted to shut her eyes and try to sleep for two hours.

She woke, rested, as the shuttle van slowed and made the turn for the ferry terminal. With only about twenty minutes before the ferry sailed, Noelle wasn't sure she would make it but set out for the walk-on passenger window.

To her surprise, she was told it was time for her to board, and she wheeled her suitcase along the ramp to the ferry.

She found an empty table with a window and slid into the seat. Moments later, the captain announced their departure, and the ferry lumbered toward the open water.

Noelle gazed out the window and realized ferry travel was her favorite method of transportation. It was slow and almost rhythmic. Plus, it provided a gorgeous view of the islands in the waters of the Salish Sea.

It was just over an hour trip, and Noelle could have stayed on the ferry for another hour. It was beyond relaxing, especially after the airport. Maybe spending the holidays tucked away on a little island wouldn't be so bad.

She made her way off the ferry and onto Front Street that ran along the harbor. Before leaving, she'd studied the map of downtown and after she took a few minutes to get her bearings, she set out for the fire station. It was less than a mile from the harbor and after sitting much of the day, Noelle was happy to stretch her legs.

Anxious to get there, she hadn't considered the added weight of her suitcase, laptop bag, and purse. It wasn't very cold and with her coat on, she was plenty warm.

She arrived at the station, a large building with a metal roof and several garage doors. She tugged her suitcase behind her to the entrance.

As she reached for the door handle, she frowned. It was locked. She noticed the sign posted with an emergency after-hours number, along with the directions to contact 911. It was a volunteer department, and the station wasn't manned full-time.

The disappointment settled over her, and the excitement she felt earlier was quickly replaced by exhaustion. She peered in the windows of the garage doors when the sound of an engine running made her turn.

She spied the big, white truck with police lights on top of it and sighed. A man in uniform with graying temples came from the driver's door and approached her. "Ma'am, I'm Sheriff Mercer. Can I help you?"

She extended her hand. "I'm Noelle Davis from Walla Walla University. I'm here to conduct an audit of the school district, but I was hoping to find someone here at the firehouse. I'm doing some research into an incident from fifty years ago."

He frowned and raised his brows. "Well, that's a few years back, isn't it?"

She sighed. "I just arrived on the ferry and walked out here. I didn't realize this was a volunteer department."

He grinned. "One of the best in the state. We do have a paid fire chief, but he's off for the day. He also wasn't around fifty years ago." He tilted his head toward the entrance. "In fact, my dad was the fire chief back then."

Noelle's eyes widened. "Really? I'd love to talk to him."

His smile faded. "Not as much as I would. He passed away a few years ago."

Noelle gasped. "I'm so sorry. I understand how hard that is. I just lost my mother a few months ago."

"My condolences," said Sheriff Mercer. "How about I give you a ride back to town? Where are you staying?"

"The Lighthouse."

He took her suitcase and laptop bag and loaded them into

the backseat. She followed, and he opened the passenger door for her. "Have a seat, and I'll get you over to the B&B."

He steered to the edge of the driveway. As he waited for a car to pass, he turned to her. "So, what is the fifty-year-old incident that brings you here?"

She let out a long breath. "I was left at the fire station as a baby on December twenty-second."

His eyes went wide. "I was only three years old at the time, but I remember my mom telling me Dad was bringing home a baby, and we were going to take care of it. He brought the baby home because it was Christmas, and there was nobody around to care for it. We were smaller back then, and Social Services was willing to let them do that."

"So, your family took care of me?"

He nodded. "I don't remember all that much, just how tiny the baby, well, you were." He pulled out onto the road.

"Do you think I could talk to your mom and see what she might remember?"

"Sure. I'll see her tonight, and we can work out something. How long are you in town?"

"I'm here until January. I have an audit to complete the first part of next week, and then I'm spending my break here. I really want to find out all I can."

He pulled up in front of the Lighthouse. "Great, I'll see what Mom has going on, and we'll set up a time." He tilted his head toward the backseat. "I'll grab your bags for you."

Back to feeling hopeful, Noelle climbed out of the truck and followed him up the steps to the reception area, where a couple was checking in. He set her bags down and tipped his hat. He pulled a business card from his pocket and handed it to her. "Here's my contact information."

She opened her handbag and slipped one of her cards from the holder and wrote her cell number on the back of it.

"Here's mine, too. Thanks so much for the ride, and I can't wait to meet your mom."

He smiled at her and slipped her card into his shirt pocket. "I'll be in touch, Ms. Davis."

"Call me Noelle, please."

"Noelle?" He grinned. "Fitting. You can call me Carson. I'll talk to you soon." He pointed at the woman behind the reception desk. "Bev will take good care of you."

She met his kind brown eyes. "Thanks, Carson. I look forward to it."

He made his way to the door, and she stepped up to the counter, where a woman wearing a cardigan greeted her with a smile. "Checking in, dear?"

Noelle smiled at her. "Yes, please." She gave Bev her name and glanced around the space while she waited, anxious to get settled.

Bev adjusted her glasses, scanned her old-school reservation book, and then turned to the computer and tapped several keys on the keyboard. Minutes later, she looked up at Noelle and shook her head. "I'm afraid I don't have a reservation for you, Ms. Davis."

Noelle's stomach knotted. "Maybe it's under Walla Walla University or the school district here? I'm doing an audit for them."

Bev nodded and continued her search. After several minutes, she removed her glasses and turned to Noelle. "I'm so sorry, I don't have anything under any of those names."

Noelle reached into her handbag and pulled out the folder Kim had given her. She plucked the reservation sheet from the papers and slid it over to the woman. "Maybe this will help. I just remembered I had a copy."

Bev tapped the logo in the corner. "Oh, I see what's

happened, dear. This is for the Lighthouse on Orcas Island. I'm afraid you're booked at the wrong island."

Noelle's head pounded. She pulled the paper closer to her and held it up so she could read it without her readers. It clearly had an Orcas Island address.

She rolled her deep-blue eyes and took a deep breath. "I'm so sorry. My assistant booked me in, and I didn't notice that. Do you happen to have a room?"

Bev shook her head. "I'm afraid we're all booked up. The holidays are one of our busiest times." She picked up a pen and added, "Let me call a couple other places for you on the off chance they'll have something." She gestured at the table with cookies and hot cider and encouraged Noelle to sit.

With her legs shaking, Noelle took her up on her offer. If Bev couldn't find her a room, she wasn't sure what to do. She nibbled on a cookie and pulled her cell phone from her purse. There were limited ferries that went from Friday Harbor to Orcas Island, and she'd just missed the last one of the day.

Her heart pounded faster, and her palms began to sweat.

As she stared at her phone, Bev touched her shoulder. "Ms. Davis, I'm sorry. Everything is full. If you leave your number, I can reach out to you if we have a cancellation."

Noelle recited her number and thanked her. Her stomach threatened to expel the few bites of the cookie she'd eaten. She collected her suitcase and dragged it out and down the steps, her hands shaking as she stood on the sidewalk.

It was already getting dark, and she had no idea where to go.

CHAPTER THREE

She zipped her coat, thankful she decided to bring a warm one, and opted to wander back toward the harbor and the ferry terminal, with the slim hope the ferry was delayed and still there. As she made her way, the cheerful lights and window displays exuded the warmth of the holidays. She noticed the twinkling lights in the window of Harbor Coffee & Books. She loved hanging out in coffee shops, and this one looked cheerful and inviting.

Noelle glanced at the empty ferry dock. Her neck ached from the stress, and tears burned in her eyes. She needed a place to think, and something warm to drink would be a comfort.

She wrestled her luggage through the door and deposited it at a table in the corner. As she waited for her large latte, the young woman behind the counter offered her a frosted brownie sprinkled with red and green decorations, on the house.

Noelle thanked her, accepted it, and took it with her drink to the table.

She pulled out her phone and looked at vacation rental sites. As she scrolled, coming up with nothing, the bells on the door jingled, and more customers arrived.

Minutes later, the sound of a man clearing his throat made her look up. Her eyes widened when she saw Sheriff Mercer standing at the edge of her table.

"Ms. Davis, I could swear I just left you at the Lighthouse. What are you doing here with all your luggage?"

She sighed and shook her head. "It's a long story."

He pointed at the chair next to hers and raised his brows.

With a gesture at the chair, she said, "Please join me."

After a sip from her cup, she relayed her predicament. "So, I'm here, hoping I can find a last-minute rental online. I honestly don't know what I'm going to do. I'm exhausted and haven't eaten all day. This is an utter mess."

Carson pulled his cell phone from his pocket. "I might have a solution. Give me a minute." He held up a finger and scrolled on his phone.

He held the phone to his ear. "Hey, Jeff. I've got a woman here. She's doing some research from fifty years ago and is a professor from Walla Walla. Long story short, her assistant booked the Lighthouse on Orcas instead of here, and now she doesn't have a place to stay. I remembered Margaret moved out of the apartment above the shop. I wondered if you and Sam might be willing to put her up in the apartment until after the first of the year?"

He nodded and smiled. "Thanks, Jeff. Her name is Noelle Davis. I'll have her text Sam her cell number so you have it."

He disconnected and grinned at her. "Done deal." He pointed at the ceiling. "Jeff's wife Sam owns this place. He's a volunteer fire fighter and friend of mine. They've got an empty furnished apartment upstairs, and it's yours for however long you need it."

The tears that had been threatening to spill fell from Noelle's eyes. She reached across the table and took his hand. "You are my hero. I don't know what to say except thank you."

"Jeff and Sam are good people. We all help each other out here on the island."

She dabbed her eyes with her napkin. "I'm happy to pay them."

He shook his head. "No need." He gave her Sam's number, and she texted her. He pointed at her bags. "Let me help you get those upstairs, and I need to pick up my pizza I ordered. You mentioned you hadn't eaten. If you're game, I'm happy to share it with you."

She laughed. "Sounds delicious, but I don't want to keep you from getting home."

"I've got no plans. I just have my girl in my vehicle."

She frowned as she tilted her head.

He laughed. "By girl, I mean my dog, Justice. She's a sweet golden retriever."

Noelle's lips curved into a wide smile, and she put her hand across her chest. "I'm relieved she's a dog. At first, I thought you meant your daughter."

He shook his head. "No kids. No wife. Just me and Justice." He pointed at the counter. "I just need to grab the key for you, and then I'll get these bags upstairs."

Before she could say anything, he was gone and within moments, she was following him up the staircase.

He opened the door and led the way in, flicking on the lights.

She took in the tidy space, with a small galley kitchen open to the living area. The inviting smell of fresh baked brownies filled the air, having drifted up from the kitchen below. She loved the soft beachy colors and accents in the throw pillows and décor. Carson pointed at a doorway. "Bedroom and bathroom are through there."

He hauled her suitcase through it, and she followed. There was even a small desk for her laptop.

She smiled. "It's perfect. Thank you again."

"My pizza should be ready." He handed her the keys to the apartment. "I'll run and get it. Be back in a few minutes."

She nodded with enthusiasm. "Yes, I'm starving."

While Carson was gone, she plugged in her cell phone to charge and noticed a reply from Sam. She smiled at the kind response letting her know to call if she had any problems. The bed had clean sheets, and there were extra towels and linens in the bathroom closet. She also asked her to be sure to lock the shop door if she left after hours. Noelle thanked her, promised to keep the door secure, and unpacked her suitcase.

As she hung up her clothes, a knock on the door drew her attention. She opened it to Carson, juggling a pizza box and another bag, but her eyes focused on the sweet-faced golden retriever holding her leash in her mouth. "Aww, you're a cutie, aren't you?" She noticed Justice and Carson shared the same gentle brown eyes.

Justice's tail arced in quick wags.

"I apologize for not asking about bringing her in but hoping you're a dog lover."

"Oh, I am. I lost my dog this summer, so I've missed out on those sweet doggie kisses and her unconditional love." She opened the door wider, and he came through and deposited their dinner on the kitchen counter. Justice followed, like his shadow.

"Aww, I'm sorry to hear about your dog. That's such a heartbreak and the worst part about having one. I'd be lost without a dog, though. Especially Justice."

"She's more than welcome. What a cutie." Noelle pointed toward the bedroom. "In fact, I saw a dog bed stashed on a shelf in the closet. I'll get it for her."

When she returned with the bed, Carson had his coat removed and their plates and silverware set up on the counter bar that separated the kitchen from the living area. "I brought salad to go with our pizza." He pointed at the container on the counter. "I don't drink soda, so I brought iced teas. Hopefully, that works for you."

"Perfect. Sounds delicious."

He pointed to the bed, and Justice hurried to it, gave it a thorough sniffing, and made herself comfy.

Noelle joined him at the counter and dug into her first cheesy slice. It and the fresh salad hit the spot.

As she reached for her cup, she sighed. "I'm feeling so much better. This is really good pizza."

"Big Tony's is the best. And the only pizza place on the island." He reached for another slice. "We have some great restaurants downtown. You won't go hungry. Also, the market is just down the street, past the hardware store. Jeff's family owns it, and he and his son Charlie run it."

"Sam texted me while you were gone. She seems lovely. I still can't believe they're willing to let a stranger stay here."

"Wait till you meet them. You'll love them."

Noelle ate two more slices and finished her salad before she announced she was stuffed.

Carson closed the lid on the box and glanced over at Justice, who was sleeping. "We better get a move on. I need to swing by Mom's and check on her on our way home."

Noelle slipped from her chair and collected their dishes. "I'm so excited to talk to your mom and see what she might remember."

As soon as Carson stood, Justice was at his side, her leash in her mouth.

"She is such a good dog." Noelle bent to pet the top of her soft head.

"She's the best. My right hand. I'm fortunate she can come to work with me." Carson smiled and motioned her to follow.

Noelle walked them to the door. "I owe you dinner for all you've done. Maybe a few dinners. I hope you'll let me repay your kindness."

With a boyish grin, he said, "I never refuse an offer of a meal. Anytime that works for you. I'll be sure to call you after I talk to Mom, and we'll set up a time for you to visit."

"That would be great." She reached for the keys on the counter. "I better walk you down so I can make sure the door is locked behind you."

He glanced at his watch. "Yeah, I think they just closed, so everyone might be gone by now."

She followed the two of them down the stairs, and they found the shop empty and dark, except for the twinkling lights in the window. She unlocked the door and watched Carson load Justice in the backseat. He turned and waved at her. "If you need anything, give me a call. My office is only a couple of blocks away."

"I will." She waved at him. "Thanks again, Carson."

He opened his door and hollered, "Get inside and lock that door. See you soon."

She did as he suggested and watched them drive away before hurrying back up the stairs.

After tidying the kitchen, she stepped into the living room and for the first time, Noelle admired the view from the window overlooking the small balcony. The colorful

Christmas lights decorating the street and harbor below were so festive.

As horrible as her day could have been, she was warm, happy, and so very grateful. Not to mention, tired. She made sure the door was locked and doused the lights before heading to the bedroom.

She was too weary to finish unpacking and put her suitcase in the corner. As she rested her head against the pillows, she closed her eyes. She was excited to learn more from Carson's mom, but before she could think further, she drifted to sleep.

CHAPTER FOUR

Noelle slept later than she had in a long time and woke to the smell of coffee on Sunday morning. The aroma prompted her to take a shower, dress, and head downstairs to procure a cup.

As she waited, she introduced herself to the barista, Yvonne, and let her know she was staying upstairs. The young woman smiled and handed her the coffee. "Sam let us know you'd be staying. Nice to meet you, Noelle. I'm sure we'll see you again."

Noelle smiled and took her coffee upstairs, where with the fresh infusion of caffeine, she mustered the energy to finish unpacking and made a list for the market.

She made her way down the quiet street to the market, where she was able to find all the staples she needed, along with a couple of bottles of wine from a display advertising a local winery. She added a couple sturdy canvas bags to make toting her groceries home easier.

As she checked out, her phone chimed with a text. It was from Sam, who gave her the Wi-Fi password and apologized for not thinking of it last night. She also let her know she'd be in the shop later in the afternoon and would love to meet her.

Noelle tapped in a reply and promised to see her later in the shop. She thanked the young man who bagged her groceries and set out for the apartment. By the time she climbed the stairs, she regretted the three bottles of wine in her bags.

She put away her groceries and filled the tea kettle to brew a cup of tea. While she waited, she logged into the wireless router and made sure her phone, laptop, and tablet worked.

When she checked her email, she saw one from her contact at the school district who offered to pick her up in the morning.

She let her know she would be at Harbor Coffee & Books and would be ready to go by seven forty-five.

As much as she wanted to dig into her abandonment fifty years ago, she forced herself to review the audit documents on her laptop and prepare for work ahead. She only had three days scheduled there, and then she'd be free to explore to her heart's content.

After making a cheese omelet and toast, she returned to her laptop. Nothing pressing from her work emails, outside of the normal reminders from administration about getting her grades turned in on time.

She emailed her assistant to let her know she wasn't staying at the Lighthouse and the confusion with the one on Orcas Island. Noelle asked her to contact them and cancel the remaining nights and get a refund. She didn't bother to berate Kim, since Noelle knew she would feel horrible enough and hopefully had learned a lesson.

With her audit documents ready and work handled,

Noelle pulled out a notepad and scribbled on it. She found the address for the library and newspaper and hoped between the two of them she might find some old articles about her being left at the fire station.

As she pondered, she wondered if her mother might still live on the island. Part of her wanted to meet her and another part of her didn't. She couldn't imagine abandoning a newborn baby. She had so many questions. She hoped she could handle the answers.

At three o'clock, Noelle went downstairs and found Sam behind the counter. The woman with her chestnut hair in a ponytail, greeted her with a warm smile. "So nice to meet you, Noelle. Do you have everything you need upstairs?"

Noelle nodded. "Oh, yes. It's beyond wonderful. Thank you for taking me in. I'm truly embarrassed about the whole situation."

Sam asked her if she'd like a drink, and Noelle opted for another one of the irresistible chai tea lattes. Sam grinned and poured milk into a container. "Well, if Carson vouches for you, it's like an automatic gold star. We're happy to help and don't give it another thought. We're not using the space and glad to help you out."

"You're very kind, and I truly appreciate it."

"Carson said you're doing some work for the school district." She handed Noelle a steaming cup and took another for herself, leading the way to a table in the corner near the bookshelves.

Noelle took a chair. "Yes, I'm a professor in Walla Walla, and we offer an audit service for governmental agencies across the state. Earlier in my career, I did more of them. It was a fun way to travel and have it paid for, and I could get some interesting case studies for my students."

"Well, that sounds like a good mix of business and pleasure."

Noelle shrugged. "Yes, I'm actually considering retirement but opted to make this trip happen. I recently found out that as a newborn, I was left at the fire station here on the island."

Sam gasped. "Oh, my gosh. That's crazy."

"I know. I had a hard time believing it. After I finish the audit, I'm hoping I can learn more about it and find my birth parents. I lost my mom a few months ago."

Sam's face softened. "I'm so sorry. I know that heartache. I lost both of my parents when I was young. I was lucky to have my grandparents."

"I'm very sorry you had to go through that." Noelle took a long sip from her cup. "I never expected to be here searching for my birth parents. I'm so intrigued to know about them, especially my mother."

Sam patted Noelle's arm. "I truly hope you find all the answers you're looking for while you're here."

"Me, too. I have to admit, I'm a little scared."

"I think that's perfectly natural. It's hard enough to lose your parents, and I can't imagine trying to come to terms with finding out you were adopted and having nobody to ask."

With a sigh, Noelle nodded. "Exactly. Then, last night when I realized I had no place to stay, I was in a real state. You and Carson came to my rescue."

"I'm just so glad we could be there for you. We're having a little get together this weekend. I hope you'll join us. We're going to gather here to watch the island's boat parade and then have dinner out at our place on Saturday."

Touched, Noelle brought her hand to her chest. "That's so sweet of you. It actually sounds like fun. I have absolutely nothing planned. My sole focus has been to find my roots, so I haven't given the holidays much thought, but I'd love to join you, if you're sure it's not an imposition."

Sam grinned and shook her head. "Not at all. We'd love to have you."

"Count me in, then," said Noelle.

Several customers walked through the door, and Sam raised her brows. "I better get back to helping at the counter. It was wonderful to meet you in person and if I don't see you before, I'll see you Saturday and introduce you to everyone."

"Sounds great. I'm looking forward to it." Noelle finished her drink and put the mug in the plastic bin on top of the trash receptacle before returning to the apartment.

Things were already looking up. She hadn't considered how lonely it would be to spend Christmas in a place where she didn't know anyone. Sam's invitation warmed her heart. Her mom always said things happened for a reason, and Noelle was beginning to believe it.

After turning in early, Noelle was dressed and ready for her audit on Monday morning. The rich aroma of coffee enticed her downstairs, where she sat with her laptop case and handbag, ready for her ride to the school district. She was almost an hour early but savored the time to relax.

As she sipped her coffee, Carson came through the door. He grinned at her and pointed at the empty chair. "I'll grab my coffee and join you if you'll be here for a few minutes."

"Please do. I have lots of time."

A few minutes later, he returned with his cup. "Looks like you're ready for work." He pointed at her suit jacket.

"Yes, my ride will be here to pick me up just before eight o'clock. I'm scheduled to work through Wednesday."

"Oh, that's great news. I talked to Mom over the weekend, and she suggested you come for dinner on Friday. Does that work for you?"

"Yes, that would be wonderful."

"I'll pick you up on my way from work, around five."

"Perfect. I'll be ready. I still owe you dinner, though. How about Wednesday night? I'm not sure if I'll have to work tonight and tomorrow but will be done for sure by then."

"Sold," he said, with a quick smile.

"You pick the place. I'm buying."

"I'll give it some thought." His radio sprang to life, and he pressed the button on his shoulder and spoke into the microphone. "I've gotta run. I'll see you Wednesday?"

"I'll be ready," she said with a smile.

He was out the door and hurrying to his truck but took the time to say hello to a couple walking on the sidewalk.

As soon as Carson left, Noelle added both dinner engagements and the get-together for the boat parade to her calendar on her phone. Then, she turned her attention to her coffee.

Moments later, a woman walked through the door and scanned the tables before smiling at Noelle. "You must be Professor Davis?" She extended her hand. "I'm Meredith Burns."

Noelle shook her hand and collected her laptop bag. "So nice to meet you and thank you for the ride this morning."

"Of course. It's on my way." She held the door for Noelle and pointed at a sedan parked in front of the store. "That's me."

Noelle settled into the passenger seat and within minutes, Meredith pulled into the small parking lot of the school district office. "I'll get you settled in the conference room and introduce you to the staff."

Once Noelle knew where to find coffee and the restrooms, she opened her laptop and began the tedious task of going through the accounting records for the last fiscal year.

She did her best to focus on her work, but the anticipation of talking to Carson's mother was hard to defy. She couldn't wait for Friday.

CHAPTER FIVE

B y Wednesday night, Noelle was tired, and her neck ached from hunching over the school district records over the last three days and two long nights. She'd stayed up late last night to complete her analysis and left Meredith with her final report just before four o'clock.

Meredith offered to drive her back downtown and left Noelle in front of Harbor Coffee & Books with a smile and her thanks for her help. "Enjoy your holidays, Professor Davis." She waved and pulled away from the curb.

With a sigh, Noelle climbed the stairs to her apartment, thankful her work obligations were over. She changed into jeans and a sweater and took a few minutes to put her feet up and decompress before Carson was due to arrive.

She scrolled her email while she sipped from the splash of wine she poured. There were several from Kim, who had been successful in getting a refund from the bed and breakfast on Orcas Island and apologized profusely for her error. She assured Noelle that all the grades had been submitted, and everything was going smoothly in her absence.

Noelle replied, thanked her, and wished her a Merry Christmas. Kim was working hard to redeem herself after the mistake with the reservations.

She put her phone down and closed her eyes. It was officially winter break, and she was free to focus on herself.

It was heavenly to sit and do nothing for a few minutes. She eyed the bottle of wine and added one more splash to her glass, making a mental note to visit the winery while she was on the island. Hopefully, they could ship her a case.

As soon as she swallowed the last sip, there was a knock on her door. She moved from the couch and answered it. Carson, dressed in jeans and a button-down shirt, stood before her. His smile went all the way to his eyes and caused the wrinkles at the corner of them to deepen. "Hope I'm not early."

"Right on time," she said. "Let me grab my coat."

He held it for her while she slipped her arms in it. She collected her purse, and they made their way downstairs. As he held the door to the shop for her, she asked, "Where are we going?"

"Have you been to Lou's yet?"

She shook her head. "No. I haven't been anywhere. The school district brought in lunch, and there was so much, I brought it home and ate leftovers for dinner the last two nights."

"Lou's is famous for all things crab, but he has an extensive menu. It's casual but very good."

"Sounds perfect to me."

He pointed toward the harbor. "We can walk. It's not far."

"Even better. I'm so tired of sitting."

She pointed at the harbor. "I love all the lights and

Christmas decorations along the railing. It's so festive. I've been enjoying the view from the balcony of the apartment."

He nodded. "We don't usually get snow, but we make up for it with all the lights and activities. Sam said you're coming to the boat parade and dinner. That's always a fun evening."

"I'm looking forward to it." He guided her toward the park next to the harbor, where they wandered the pathway and took in the trees wrapped in white lights.

They made the last turn, and the huge town Christmas tree twinkling with colorful lights came into view. She gasped when she saw it. "Wow, that is gorgeous."

"It's one of the best things about living here. Mom and Dad were always big on Christmas and coming to the tree lighting was a huge deal for our family." They gazed at the sparkling tree for a few minutes, then wandered back to the street.

He tilted his head at the restaurant perched with a view of the harbor below. "We're here."

They climbed the stairs, and Carson introduced her to Andi, Lou's significant other who also worked part-time at the hospital. She greeted them with a warm smile and led them to a table near the windows.

Noelle studied the menu. She was starving, and everything looked good. Andi highlighted the special new charcuterie boards they were featuring, and they opted to order one for an appetizer.

When the server returned with a glass of the same wine Noelle had been enjoying earlier and iced tea for Carson, they were ready to order. They both settled on burgers with crab mac and cheese for their dinner. Moments later, Andi appeared with their appetizer.

Noelle pointed to her wine glass. "This is really good. I

found it at the market and was intrigued since it's a local winery."

"They have a great venue. You'll have to go out and see it. Blake and Ellie own it, but his family is big in the wine business in Yakima, I think."

"We've got some great wineries in the Walla Walla area, too. I've been to Yakima a few times. I'll definitely make a point of visiting this one."

Noelle dug into the savory bites of cheese and as she nibbled, she felt better. Carson finished off a slice of cheese on a cracker. "So, how was your last day at the school district?"

"Long," she said, reaching for some grapes. "I've been working at night to make sure to get it done but turned in my final report right before I left. Everyone was very nice there."

"How often do you travel to do audits?"

She laughed. "This is the first one I've done in about twenty years. The college has a long history of giving back to smaller local government agencies, and it gives staff and even students opportunities to learn from the real world or use the audits as case studies in the classroom. I used to do them all the time but was only enticed to come here because of my history and quest to find my roots."

"Sounds like it was meant to be."

She raised her brows. "Exactly what I thought. I've really been struggling with the loss of my mom and this news that I only learned about after she was gone. I took it as a sign I needed to come here." She took a sip of wine. "Enough about me. How is your week going?"

He sat back in his chair and sighed. "It's always a busy time of year with lots of holiday activities. We always coordinate a local toy drive and a donation drive to gather items for seniors in the community. Not to mention a party we coordinate to distribute the gifts collected. My sergeant, who is the point person, had a family emergency come up today, and he and his wife have to travel. He'll be gone the rest of the year, so I had that added to my plate."

The busser stopped by and refilled his iced tea and both their water glasses. He thanked the young man. "We're a small department, so we all wear quite a few hats. We'll manage, it's just a bump in the road."

Noelle shrugged. "I'm happy to help. I don't have much to do other than my research, but I'm sure I can squeeze in some time to volunteer. Tomorrow, I planned to visit the newspaper office and library and see if there are any birth records at the local hospital that might help."

"The newspaper office is further down the road from the fire station. How about I loan you my car while you're here? I always drive my patrol unit, so it wouldn't be a problem. That way you don't have to walk everywhere."

She shook her head. "I don't want to put you out. I don't mind walking."

"It's no bother. I've got a truck and a car, and they're both just sitting in the garage. I try to drive them on the weekends, so I keep their batteries charged. You'd be doing me a favor, putting a few miles on one or both of them."

"Just give me the one you care the least about. I'm a good driver, but I don't want to scratch something you love."

"Definitely the car. It's just a plain old car. My truck is one I got in high school. It's special."

She laughed. "Definitely not the truck. I'll do better with a car. I'm not used to anything big."

"Consider it done. I'll drop it by your place tomorrow morning."

The waiter arrived with their entrees and took away the

almost empty charcuterie board. "This looks so good," said Noelle, as she dug into the creamy mac and cheese.

After prepping his burger, he glanced across the table. "Back to your offer to help out with the donation drives. If you're serious, we'll take you up on that. It would be a huge help."

"I'm serious. I'm in. Just show me the ropes."

"If it works, I'll drop my car by, then we can go to my office, and I'll give you a rundown, plus all the historical files so you can get a feel for what's been done in the past years."

"Sounds perfect. That will give me something to do between searching for my past."

"Hopefully, Mom remembers something helpful. She's still sharp."

"Oh, speaking of your mom. Is there anything I can bring to dinner? Does she like wine or dessert?"

He raised his brows. "She's not much for wine, and I don't drink at all, but dessert would be great. Sam makes delicious pies, and Sweet Treats, the bakery down the street, is also very good."

"Great, let her know I'll bring dessert. I appreciate you going to all this trouble. I'm sure you have better things to do."

He chuckled. "As a matter of fact, I'm enjoying getting to know you. I tend to be a workaholic and don't have much of a social life. It's been nice to do something other than work late and go home to fall asleep watching television."

Noelle took a sip from her wine glass. "Sounds like you're also living the dream."

They both laughed. "You could say that. I lead a boring life, I guess."

"I think it's just a matter of getting into a routine that works. Sometimes boring is nice. I could use a little boring, in fact. I've had a rough time since my daughter Courtney went to college back east. She's been my whole world ever since my husband died when she was young. Losing Mom, not to mention my sweet dog, has left me feeling adrift this past year. Along with the news I was adopted, I've been on overwhelm. I'm actually looking forward to spending the holidays here instead of alone at home."

"I like routine, too. I'm sorry you've had a rough patch. Losing my dad a few years ago put me into a tailspin, and I can't even think about losing my mom. The island is a special place, especially during the holidays."

"Being a grown up is not all it's cracked up to be, is it?"

He shook his head. "No, it's not." He looked out the window. "I think that's what I enjoy about the holidays. It brings back those wonderful childhood memories."

"Do you have brothers and sisters?" she asked, loading her fork with more mac and cheese.

"I'm the baby. I have an older brother and sister. They don't live on the island, and both have their own families. We thought they might come for Christmas this year, but it's not going to work out. They were here for Thanksgiving though, which was great for Mom."

"Courtney came home for Thanksgiving, too. She surprised me with the news that she got engaged." Noelle raised her brows. "So, there's that."

"I take it you're not excited about your new son-in-law?"

She wrinkled her nose. "It's not that. I just think they're too young. Phil seems nice. I've only met him once when I went back for a visit. I had no idea it was serious at that point. His family is wealthy and are always kind to Courtney and include her in their celebrations. They live in Connecticut, have a vacation home in Vermont." She shook her head. "I can't compete with all that."

He reached across the table and put his hand on top of hers. "Don't sell yourself short, Noelle. Young people always think they know best, and I doubt Courtney is trying to slight you. She's just excited about the next step in her life and might not understand you're not quite ready for it."

Tears formed in her eyes, and she blinked several times, focusing on the flame of the votive candle on their table and the view beyond it out the window. She was afraid if she met Carson's kind brown eyes, she'd lose it.

CHAPTER SIX

The next morning, Noelle slept late and dawdled over a cup of tea. After too many glasses of wine last night, she was drowsy and asked Carson to come with the car at ten o'clock so she wouldn't be rushed.

With the late hours she'd put in on the audit, she needed extra sleep.

Once she was showered and ready, she made her way downstairs for a latte. She found Sam behind the counter, where they chatted for a few minutes, and Noelle ordered a pie to take to Carson's mother's house for tomorrow night.

Sam winked when Noelle told her where she was taking the pie. "Betty is a huge fan of my berry cheesecake pie. I'll do that one for you." She wrote out an order slip, and Noelle paid her for it and her latte.

"I'll pick it up tomorrow afternoon." Noelle took a sip from her chai tea latte. "I'm addicted to these. They are so good."

"I love them, too," said Sam. "Since you'll have a loaner car, if you can't find a parking spot, you can pull in behind the building or park behind the hardware store. Either one works."

"Thanks, I'll be sure to do that." Noelle glanced out the window where Carson was walking toward the door. "There's my ride now."

He came through the door and smiled, greeting several of the customers on his way to the counter. "Hey, Sam," he said, stepping beside Noelle. "I need to steal Noelle away."

"She's all yours. See you two later," she said, waving as they made their way to the door.

He handed her the keys and pointed to the brown sedan in front of the shop. "You can drive us back to the office and get a feel for her."

She slid behind the wheel and adjusted the mirrors. A trace of nervousness made her pulse quicken. She glanced over at him. "I feel like I'm back taking my driver's test."

He laughed. "Ah, don't worry. I'm an easy grader."

She pulled away from the curb, and he directed her to the turn that would lead them to his office, just two blocks from the coffee shop. Minutes later, unscathed, she parked in the lot of the brick building, where he pointed.

"Come on in, and I'll show you the files for the donation drives. I also printed out a map for you, so you know where to go for the newspaper, library, and hospital."

"Wow, thanks. That's helpful."

She followed him in the door that required a keycard to enter, and he led her through a hallway to his office. As soon as he reached his desk, a woman with short red hair came through another door on the side of Carson's office.

"Sheriff, I've got a couple of urgent messages for you." She handed him a slip of paper.

"Thanks, Joan." He gestured toward Noelle. "This is Noelle Davis. She's a professor from Walla Walla visiting for the holidays and volunteered to help coordinate the donation drives and party with Fred being out."

Joan, who wore lipstick that matched her hair and green sparkly eyeshadow that matched her shirt, smiled and extended her hand. "Aren't you an angel? Pleasure to meet you."

"Nice to meet you, too."

Carson gestured toward Joan. "Joan is my right hand here. If you need anything, just ask her. She knows everything and if she doesn't, she'll find someone who does."

Joan moved her head toward the door that led to the hallway. "Come with me, and I'll show you all the important places."

Noelle left her coat and handbag on the chair in front of Carson's desk and followed Joan into the hallway.

She took a turn and pointed at a door. "The all-important ladies room."

Noelle nodded and followed Joan further down the hallway past a room outfitted with tables and whiteboards. On the next left, Joan stopped. "Here's the break room. Vending machines, coffee, tea, water, microwave, and fridge. Even an oven if you need one." Joan pointed at a bakery box on the counter. "Anything on the counter is fair game. If you bring something and put it in the fridge or a cabinet, just label it with your name. If you disguise it as a salad, all the better. Nobody accidentally eats those."

She laughed and continued the tour, pointing out other offices that Noelle doubted she would remember. She circled back to the hallway where Carson's office was and turned right, where she stepped into a small office that smelled like cinnamon, decorated with silk flowers, knickknacks, and photographs. "This is my office."

Joan pointed to the door in the corner of it. "That leads to the conference room off Sheriff Mercer's office." She picked up a business card from the holder on her desk and wrote on it. "Here's my cell number, and my direct line is on the front. If you need anything at all, just give me a shout."

Noelle slipped it in the pocket of her jeans, next to her cell phone. "Thanks, Joan. I'm sure I'll have to reach out to you until I get the hang of things."

"Not to worry," she said, opening the door in the corner. "I'm sure Sheriff Mercer will want you to set up in here. I'll get you some basic supplies and make sure there's enough empty space in the file cabinet for you to store your files. When you leave, just put everything in there. That way, if we need to use the room, we won't risk disturbing your files."

"Got it," said Noelle.

"One more thing, if that light above the door that leads to his office is red, that means he's busy and can't be disturbed. You can always come and go through my office anytime."

Noelle nodded. "Understood. Thanks so much for showing me around."

"You bet. I'll let Sheriff Mercer walk you through the files, but I'm happy to help. I usually pitched in and helped Fred with the project, too."

"Wonderful news. It will take me a bit to get acclimated, but I'm determined to make it a success."

Joan winked at Noelle, her fake eyelashes locking together. "I'm sure you will. This holiday project is very important to Sheriff Mercer, so I know he wouldn't put it in your hands if he didn't trust you."

Joan opened the door into Carson's office and left Noelle with a promise to be back soon with her office supplies and a visitor keycard so she could come and go as she needed.

Carson hung up the phone and smiled at her. He pointed at the small table across from his desk. "I've got the files ready for you. I can walk you through them, and then I've got to get to a meeting."

"Works for me. Joan gave me the tour and once I get organized here, I'll head out to make my inquiries and come back later to get to work."

"Perfect." He carried the stack of folders and led the way to the conference room.

Noelle's eyes widened. "Joan is efficient." She pointed at the sticky notes, pens, notepads, and highlighters sitting next to the lanyard with the visitor pass.

Carson grinned. "That she is. She's not everyone's cup of tea, but she does a great job, and I'd be lost without her. She's also very loyal and despite her chatty banter, knows how to keep things confidential."

He took a chair next to Noelle and opened the first file. "This is a list of local businesses and residents who donate to the project, along with their contact information. Joan already sent letters out earlier in the month, so you'll just need to follow up on that. We're behind this year, so time is of the essence."

He explained that in addition to the large bins in their lobby and the main entrance to the county offices, several local businesses had collection barrels for toys and items for local seniors. "This list shows where they are and the point of contact. You'll need to arrange to collect them toward the end of next week in time for the big party we have to distribute them. We use the senior center for the party each year, usually in the morning before they serve lunch. We distribute the toys at the firehouse, which you'll be visiting today anyway. It's usually the day school gets out in the afternoon to make it easy for parents to stop by after work. The biggest thing you'll need to coordinate is the gift wrapping and securing a Santa for the kids' party."

Noelle scribbled notes while he went through the main points.

His desk phone rang out, and he excused himself. Noelle flipped through the papers in the file. Fred was organized, and it looked like it would be easy to replicate.

She made a few more notes on her notepad and then put the files in the drawer Joan had cleared for her.

As she gathered her things, Carson came through the door. "Sorry about that. Looks like you're heading out?"

"Yeah, I'm going to hit up those places this morning, but I'll be back later to work on things. I've got a list of things to check."

"Terrific. I'll catch up with you later when you're back."

She promised to update him and left through Joan's office, where Noelle asked her to provide a list of the replies she'd received to the initial email sent to donors.

Joan nodded. "I'll get that to you in a spreadsheet. I found you a laptop to use and set up a temporary email for you here so you can send and receive things. It will be in your inbox by the time you get back." She handed her a card with her email and temporary password. "I'll have the laptop ready by then, too."

"Perfect, thanks so much, Joan. See you later this afternoon." Noelle made her way through the hallway and out to the car.

As much as she was anxious to learn more about how she ended up left at the fire station, Noelle pulled out of the parking lot, happy to have a project to keep her busy while she was searching. Part of her knew it was a longshot that she'd find anything, and she was grateful to have something to occupy her time. Especially something as worthy as a project helping seniors and kids.

CHAPTER SEVEN

She'd studied the map Carson gave her and knew the route to get to the fire station and newspaper. She parked along the street and walked to the entrance of the station, where a young firefighter greeted her.

Noelle introduced herself and said she was researching an event from fifty years ago and was hoping she might be able to talk to someone or look at any records they might have when a baby was left at the station, abandoned.

The firefighter's eyes widened. "Let me get Chief Allison for you. He'd be your best bet."

He picked up a phone on the wall, and his request for Chief Allison blared over the intercom system. "I'll take you to his office, where you can wait for him." He led her down a hallway to a large office with a couch along the wall and two chairs in front of a desk piled with notes and papers, blueprints, and a computer.

After declining his offer of something to drink, he left her to wait.

She perused the walls, filled with old black and white

photos depicting various fires. As she studied them, a tall man came through the door. "Ms. Davis, sorry to keep you waiting. I'm Chief Allison."

Noelle's shoulders drooped when she saw he looked to be her age or younger but shook his hand and explained her dilemma. His forehead creased, and he tilted his head. "That era would have been under Chief Mercer. I'm afraid he's passed away."

"Yes, I actually ran into his son when I came here this weekend in the hopes of finding someone who might remember."

"This wasn't even the fire station back then. Friday Harbor had their own volunteer department, and it was downtown on West Street. They merged with the San Juan County Fire over twenty years ago."

She wrote down the address of the old fire station on her notepad. "Are there any other firefighters who would have been around back then, still on the island?"

"Hmm, let me do some research. We've got some old rosters and such in storage. I can see what I can find and narrow that down for you. I've only been here about ten years, so I'm not as familiar with the history and am trying to think of anyone who might know more."

He made a note and wrote her phone number and name on one of the many tablets strewn across his desk. As he handed her his card, he said, "You know, one person you might ask is Jeff Cooper. He has Cooper Hardware downtown; he's a volunteer here, and his dad was, too. His dad is of the right generation. I know he's passed away, but Jeff might be able to come up with someone who might remember. His family has been here for generations."

"Thanks for the tip. I'm helping coordinate the toy drive for Christmas, so I'll be talking to him anyway. Speaking of that, do you have a few minutes to discuss the logistics of the party and show me how it's usually done?"

He nodded. "Sure. Come with me, and I'll show you where we set up."

He led her to a large multipurpose room off the kitchen. "We set up cookies and cocoa in here for the kids and anyone else who wants it. If memory serves, we open the doors at three o'clock, after school is out for the day."

With a nod, she made a note. He confirmed the firefighters handle serving and stocking the cookies and cocoa. "Do you provide the treats, or do we need to order that?"

"Oh, we handle it. We donate all of that from our fundraising." He motioned her to follow him and showed her the large area where the trucks were parked. "We move out the trucks and set up Santa in here."

The space was huge, and she imagined it could fit every kid who lived on the island and more. "I reviewed the past files, and it looks like we deliver bins of wrapped toys and separate them by age group and boys and girls, so Santa can give an age-appropriate gift."

Chief Allison nodded. "Right. We recruit a few elves, in costume of course, from our ranks to help Santa out with that. As long as your bins are marked, and we explain that to Santa's helpers, we should be set."

With a sigh, Noelle smiled. "Well, you're making this too easy. I'll make sure that happens and will also make sure Santa is here by two o'clock."

He guided her back to the entrance. She shook his hand, and he promised to be in touch if he found any information.

She set out down the road for the local newspaper office. Just past a car wash, two log buildings with green metal roofs appeared, and Noelle turned into the shared parking lot for the complex.

After consulting the signage, she made her way to the office of the *Journal.* Behind the door, Noelle found a quiet office with a counter and two desks, neither of which were occupied.

The aroma of coffee lingered in the air, but that was the only sign of life in the barebones operation.

As Noelle contemplated stepping behind the counter to see if she could find anyone, a woman came from around the corner. "Hello, so sorry. I didn't hear you come in."

Noelle smiled and introduced herself. "I'm researching an event that happened fifty years ago and was hoping you might have old copies of the newspaper or electronic images I could search."

The young woman shook her head. "We don't have them here, but the historical society maintains our collection and that of the *Friday Harbor Journal* and the *San Juan Islander*, both of which operated during that timeframe."

"Wonderful. What's their address?"

The young woman wrote it on a piece of paper. "It's just a couple minutes down the road. They're open until two o'clock and closed on Sundays and Mondays. The best person to help you is a woman named Bunny. She's been there for years."

"Thanks so much," said Noelle. "I appreciate your help."

She took the address and climbed behind the wheel of Carson's car. The address led her to a white two-story clapboard house. She parked in the almost empty lot and climbed the steps to the entry door.

A friendly woman wearing a volunteer badge welcomed her.

Noelle returned her smile. "I was just at the newspaper office and am looking for Bunny. I have a research project."

The woman smiled and nodded. "Bunny's the best. Let me see if she's at her desk." She picked up a phone and after a quick conversation, walked closer to Noelle and pointed at a hallway. "Just take that hallway. She's in the last office on the left."

"Thanks," said Noelle, anxious to make her way to the promise of some information.

Upon entering the office, she found a desk piled with folders, thick leather-bound books, and photographs. She stood taller and peered over the stacks where a curly gray head of hair bent over a notepad. The woman looked up and chuckled. "Welcome to my cave," she said.

Noelle smiled. "You must be Bunny."

"Yes," she said, standing. "Let's chat over at the conference table, and you can tell me how I can help you."

Noelle followed the petite woman to a large wooden table tucked into a space between bookcases and filing cabinets overflowing with material. Bunny gestured to a chair, and Noelle took a seat.

She explained about finding out she was adopted and left as a baby at the fire station fifty years ago, right before Christmas. "I actually ran into Sheriff Mercer, and he remembers his dad, who was the fire chief at the time, bringing home a baby to take care of until the people at social services could find someone."

Bunny nodded. "I remember when that happened." She shook her head. "I don't recall ever hearing much more about it. It was just such a sad thing to have happen during the holidays, so it got some attention."

"I thought there might be some articles in the newspaper

that would help or give me a clue as to who might have left me. I'd like to know my birth mother."

Bunny's eyes softened behind her glasses. "I'm sure you would, dear. Let's see what we can find in the archives."

She led Noelle through a doorway and into another hallway and finally a large room without windows. Deep shelves lined two walls, and a large wooden table filled the center of the room.

Bunny turned on a lamp and wandered over to one of the shelves. "We've got the really old stuff on microfilm, but what you're after will be in these bound volumes." She pointed at a stack on the shelf, and Noelle helped her pull the one lettered 1974 to the table.

Bunny went back and ran her finger over the gold letters on the spine until she found the volume with the first part of 1975. "We'll take this one too, just in case there was anything written after the first of the year."

Once they placed the other volume on the table, Bunny opened a drawer and removed a pair of white gloves. "These volumes aren't really properly preserved, but I still like to take precautions and not touch the delicate newsprint. It's very fragile."

With great care, she opened the 1974 volume to the last section and carefully turned the pages until she found the editions from late December. "They published the paper twice a week back then." She pointed to the date of December 27. "News wasn't like today. It wasn't instantaneous."

Noelle scanned the headlines on the yellowed paper. Most of them were linked to the holiday celebrations and services in the community. With gentle movements, Bunny turned each page as they continued to scan all the articles.

With a gloved finger, Bunny drew Noelle's attention to

the local statistics where the paper printed births, marriages, and deaths each week. "There was just a small clinic on the island then, not the hospital we have today. Many babies were born on the ferry or in Bellingham."

No births were shown for December twenty-first.

"There were a couple of midwives who delivered babies, but they would have registered the birth." Bunny pointed at the 1975 volume. "It looks like with the holidays, that was the last edition of the year. Let's see what we learn in the next edition of the paper."

Noelle replaced the heavy volume on the shelf while Bunny opened the next one. They scanned the first two editions of the paper and found no mention of a baby left at the fire station and no record of a birth on December twenty-first.

Feeling deflated, Noelle put the thick volume back on the shelf and sighed. "Thank you for helping me look."

Bunny put the gloves back in the drawer. "I'm sorry we didn't find anything. I can send an information request to the hospital in Bellingham and see if they have birth records from December twenty-first. They aren't quick about it, but eventually, I'll get an answer."

"Wow, that would be terrific. I had the hospital on my list to check with today."

Bunny's gray curls bounced as she shook her head. "They won't be able to help you at all. They don't have any records that go back that far. They've only been on the island a few years now."

"If you're willing, I'd be grateful. That will save me a trip and lots of phone calls since I wouldn't know where to start in Bellingham."

"I'll send it out today. Of course, Bellingham isn't the only hospital on the mainland; it's just the closest one to the ferry landing that most women took. In reality though, you could have been born in Seattle or Tacoma, or a few other cities."

"I have to start somewhere, and Bellingham sounds like a good lead." She left Bunny with her contact information and let her know she was staying in town until January. "Thanks again for your help, Bunny."

"My pleasure, dear. I hope you find what you're looking for and Merry Christmas."

With a less hopeful spring in her step than when she'd arrived, Noelle found her way back to the entrance and set out for Carson's office.

This quest would be harder than she thought.

CHAPTER EIGHT

After spending two days immersed in organizing the toy and donation drive for the seniors, Friday afternoon, Noelle stashed her files in the cabinet, wished Joan a happy weekend, and headed for her apartment.

She had more than two hours before she was due for dinner at Carson's mother's house and opted to grab a latte and take a walk by the harbor park to enjoy the Christmas tree. With a nearby bench empty, she took a seat and gazed at the tree with the water beyond. Several boats were decked out with lights, and the picturesque view was one she would miss when she had to go back to Walla Walla.

In an odd twist of fate, she remembered her mom talking about taking a trip to the San Juan Islands, and tears dotted her cheeks. She should have made the time to make that happen. Her mom would have loved this.

After she finished her latte, she strolled back to the coffee shop and picked up the pie she'd ordered. She carried the box upstairs and found a note with her name on it stuck to her door. She unlocked the door so as not to chance dropping the pie and as soon as she opened it, the fragrance of Christmas wafted from it.

She stepped inside and set the pie on the counter and opened the note. It was from Sam and Jeff. They apologized for going into the apartment but wanted her to have a tree for the season.

Noelle took in the gorgeous tree, stationed to the side of the window in the living room. Tears filled her eyes and blurred the twinkling lights strung in the branches. They'd even decorated it with pretty Christmas balls and glass snowflakes. It was beyond beautiful.

The tree was one of her favorite things about Christmas, but when Courtney broke the news that she wouldn't be home, Noelle hadn't bothered with one. Without her and her beloved mom, it didn't seem like Christmas. Being on the island for the holidays, she hadn't even given it a thought.

Her heart filled with joy at the sight and at the thoughtfulness of Sam and Jeff. After striking out with the newspapers, Noelle thought she might not find her birth mother, but even if she didn't, she'd found the warmth of friendship and community on the tiny island, and that meant the world to her.

Noelle debated about what to wear to dinner. Her options were slim. She brought mostly jeans, sweaters, and a few blouses, along with the pantsuits she wore to conduct the audit. A suit didn't feel like the right choice.

She opted for jeans and a deep-blue blouse that matched her eyes. As she slipped a pair of hoop earrings in her ears, a soft knock on her door drew her attention.

She hurried to answer it and found Carson. "I just need to grab the pie and my coat, and I'm ready."

"No rush." He stepped inside and pointed at the tree. "Wow, you've been busy. Your tree looks great."

She shrugged. "That's all thanks to Jeff and Sam. They surprised me with it while I was gone today."

He offered to carry the pie, and they descended the stairs. He held the passenger door of his patrol truck open for her and handed her the pie once she was settled. "Don't let Justice sweet talk you into a bite."

At the sound of her name, Justice popped her head between the two front seats. Noelle reached over to pet her while Carson slid behind the wheel. He drove less than a mile and turned onto a quiet street.

He carried the pie, and Justice followed them as he led the way to a cute blue and white cottage-style home. He rang the bell, and the door opened in seconds. A woman with short, white hair smiled at them.

Carson motioned Noelle through the door. "Mom, this is Noelle Davis. My mom, Betty Mercer."

Betty, with an apron over her blouse and jeans, reached out and hugged Noelle. "I'm so happy you're here. Please come in. Dinner is about ready for us."

Carson carried the pie into the kitchen and sniffed. "Smells like my favorite lasagna."

Betty laughed and rolled her eyes. "He's a hoot, isn't he?"

"Can I do anything to help, Mom?"

"You can carry that lasagna for me. It must weigh twenty pounds."

As the two of them worked in the kitchen, and Justice lounged on the dog bed in the corner of the living room, Noelle admired the family photos stashed on every surface in the living room.

One at Christmas, with Carson and his siblings, along with their parents in front of the town tree by the harbor touched Noelle's heart. They were all smiling and decked out in holiday sweaters and shirts. She wondered if that had been one of their last family photos when all of them lived on the island together.

"I think we're set," said Betty. "I've got iced tea or water. What would you like, Noelle?"

Noelle tugged herself away from the lure of old photos and joined the two of them at the small dining table situated off the kitchen. "Either works for me."

Carson poured her iced tea from the pitcher and pulled out her chair.

Noelle eyed the huge lasagna and savored the aroma of garlic bread coming from the basket next to her. Carson dished up squares of lasagna for each of them, and Betty passed her the salad.

After adding a thick slice of garlic bread to her plate, Noelle cut into the steaming lasagna but opted to let it cool before digging into it. Carson didn't hold back and took a forkful. "Mmm, I'm starving, and this is so good, Mom."

She beamed at the compliment. "Thank you. I figured you'd be happy with your favorite."

Noelle added a small helping to her fork and followed it with a bite of garlic bread. "It is delicious, Mrs. Mercer."

"Oh, call me Betty, please. We're not fancy around here, and I'm delighted you like it."

As they ate, Carson brought up the topic Noelle was itching to discuss. "So, Mom, you said you remembered the baby girl Dad brought home all those years ago."

She chuckled. "Yes, it was the first and only time he found a baby at the door of the fire station. It was quite memorable." She glanced across the table at Noelle. "I can't believe you're that baby. It's incredible."

Noelle smiled at her. "Believe me, it was quite shocking to learn I was adopted and even more to find out I was left at the fire station. I'm just hoping to find my birth mother or at least know who she was."

Betty's jaw tightened. "Carson told me you were hoping for that. I'm afraid I have no idea who your birth mother was. We never heard a whisper of a theory. At that time, we were all curious, but we focused on taking care of you the best we could and getting you through the holidays."

She went on to tell Noelle that she dressed her in the baby clothes she had from Carson and his siblings, and several of the ladies at the church pitched in and provided everything she didn't have, with one of them even making Noelle a Christmas outfit.

Betty's eyes filled with tears. "Part of me hated to see you go when the lady from child services came after Christmas and picked you up. You were a special gift for us that year."

She paused and added. "I never told anyone this, but I had a miscarriage earlier that year, and the doctor said I couldn't have any more children. You, coming to stay with us, was such a joyful time, and you helped heal my broken heart."

Carson's eyes went wide. "How come you never told me that, Mom?"

She shook her head and glanced over at him. "It's not something that comes up in normal conversation. It was just one of those things that happened, and we powered through it."

Noelle used her napkin to dab at her eyes. "Oh, I'm so very sorry that happened."

Betty smiled. "Don't be sorry. Like I said, you were such a cute little bundle to have around for Christmas. Frank and I even discussed the idea of adopting you, but by the time we decided, it was too late, and they'd already found parents for you. We, of course, wanted to know more about you, but they told us they couldn't divulge any information."

Noelle brought her hand to her chest. "Aww, that is so sweet. Thankfully, I had wonderful parents. I lost my mom earlier this year, and it's been so hard."

They finished their meal, with Betty sharing stories of the past. "I actually went through my old photos and found a few of you when you were with us that year. I took them to the drugstore and got copies made of them for you."

Carson volunteered to take care of the dishes and left the two of them to reminisce. Betty led her into the living room and handed Noelle an envelope.

Betty pointed at the recliner on the other side of hers and turned on the lamp between them. I'll get us some tea, and you can start looking."

Noelle opened the large envelope and pulled out the stack of photos that were clipped together. The first one was of a tiny baby with a striped pink and white hat in a plastic carrier. Bits of dark hair poked out from the cap on her head.

Betty arrived with mugs of tea and took her seat. Justice settled in at her feet. "We had the local doctor check you out, and he pronounced you healthy. We quizzed him, hoping he might know the mother, but he had no patients that had given birth or were that far along."

The next photo showed the baby inside the fire station, where a man was smiling and holding her. Betty pointed at it. "That's my Frank."

Next came one with a red plastic fire hat resting atop her carrier. The hat was bigger than the baby.

All the rest of the photos were of Noelle at the Mercers' house. They posed with her in front of their tree, and several were of Betty holding her and rocking her. It was easy to see the love and bond Betty formed with the tiny girl.

Noelle smiled at the one with Carson, a toddler, and his siblings, all sitting on the couch and his older sister cradling the baby. She gasped at the one with a Christmas outfit, complete with a tiny Santa hat.

With tears in her eyes, Noelle looked over at Betty, whose cheeks were also wet. "Thank you for taking such good care of me. I was so lucky Frank was the one to find me."

Betty reached across the table separating the two chairs and gripped Noelle's hand. "It was my absolute pleasure. Like I said, you were a gift, and I believe God sent you to me that year to help heal my shattered heart."

With a smile, Noelle pointed at the photos. "I'll treasure these. Thank you for taking the time to make copies for me."

Carson came from the kitchen with his own mug of tea and took a seat on the sofa. He gestured to the photos in Noelle's hand. "Mom showed me those earlier. Pretty cute, huh?"

"Very." He smiled and took a long sip from his mug. "If you ladies are ready for pie, I'm happy to cut and serve."

With a chuckle, Betty grinned at her son. "That's Carson's way of saying he's ready for pie."

He raised his brows at her. "Did Noelle tell you it's your favorite berry cheesecake from Sam's?"

Betty slapped her hands on her knees. "Well, that changes things. Of course, I'm ready."

Carson sprang into action and delivered plates with slices of pie and poured more tea for everyone. As they dug into the luscious pie, Noelle asked more questions about her early days on the island.

"Did you ever have an inkling who might have been my birth mother, Betty?

She shook her head. "No. Frank and I gave it so much thought, and we didn't know anyone who was expecting. We finally settled on the theory that it must have been someone who came to the island, left you at the station, and then took the next ferry out. We suspected she must have had a tie to the island or a reason for coming here, but we never figured it out."

"I'm interested in talking to anyone who lived here at the time and might have a lead or idea. If you can think of anyone you remember from then that still lives here, I'd love to talk to them."

Betty's eyes widened. "I'll give that some thought."

"No rush. I'm just grasping at straws at this point."

Carson collected their empty plates and took them to the kitchen. "Thanks for dinner, Mom. I know you turn in early, so we won't keep you up late."

He bent and hugged her. "Oh, it's been wonderful to have you both here."

Noelle also thanked her and couldn't resist hugging her. "I appreciate all this so much, Betty."

She walked them to the door and as they were putting on their jackets, Betty raised her hand. "Oh, I almost forgot. Carson tells me you're taking the reins on the donation drives for the holidays. I talked to the ladies at my church, and we're all ready to help wrap, so just let us know where and when, and we'll be there."

Noelle's smile widened. "That's wonderful news. I just talked to the fire chief this afternoon and reserved the firehouse for the wrapping party. I'll get the details to you. That will be wonderful to have all that help."

As they stepped outside, they noticed the rain showering over them. Carson reached back inside and returned with a tan felt hat, similar to the style he wore as part of his uniform. He handed it to Noelle. "This will keep the rain off your head." He hugged his mother goodbye and reminded her to lock her door.

He loaded Justice into the backseat and held the door for Noelle before climbing into the driver's seat. Within a few minutes, they were back in front of Sam's coffee shop, which was still open. He hopped out and over her objections, walked her to the door of her apartment.

She unlocked the door and smiled at him. "Have a good night, Carson, and thanks so much for introducing me to your mom. It was a wonderful evening."

"She's been looking forward to it all week. I'll see you tomorrow at the boat parade, if not before."

"I'm so excited to attend. It sounds like fun." She plucked the hat from her head and handed it to him.

He shook his head. "Keep it, you might need it again."

She waved goodbye as he descended the steps and chuckled when he hollered out to remind her to lock her door, too.

She hung his hat on the coat rack by the door. He was a good guy. She hadn't dated or even tried to date in a very long time. He was the kind of man she wished she would have met years ago. She would miss him when she left to go home.

CHAPTER NINE

Saturday morning, Noelle was up early and working, drafting the email to solicit wrappers from the staff at the sheriff's department and the fire department. Both groups had volunteered in the past. She also sent a personal email to Betty with the particulars and thanked her for rallying her church group. With them and the volunteers from the departments, Noelle hoped they would make quick work of the task. She sent it along to Joan to send from their main email account.

She checked her notes and still on her to-do list was the contact point at the senior center. Jeff from the hardware store was also on that list. She made her way downstairs, grabbed a latte, and walked across the street.

Clouds hung in the sky, but the rain was gone, leaving that wonderful, fresh smell in its wake.

As she came through the door of Cooper Hardware, she found Jeff in an aisle, helping a customer find something. As soon as he was done, he smiled at her. "Morning, Noelle. What can we help you with?"

"Actually, I was looking for you. First, I have to thank you for the gorgeous tree in the apartment. I love it, and you and Sam were very thoughtful to think of me."

"Everybody needs a tree." He winked at her.

"I'm also working on the donation drives, and the old notes tell me you played a vital role."

He chuckled. "It's one of my favorite projects. We're happy to retrieve the donation barrels and bring them here for sorting. Everyone who works here pitches in, and we have pizza and make it a fun event. I've already got all the wrapping paper and supplies here. We always donate those."

"That's terrific and so kind. Collecting the barrels is a huge job, and I appreciate your willingness to do that. I've got the firehouse reserved for a wrapping party on Wednesday for the toys and Saturday for the items for the seniors. The party for the kids is on Friday at three o'clock."

He nodded. "Okay, we'll pick up the toys on Monday and get them sorted and wait until Wednesday to collect the other items. We just group like items together for the seniors. We get loads of socks, slippers, blankets, along with personal care items."

"Perfect. I'll send out an email to all the locations to let them know, and we'll blast that on social media and encourage all the vendors to do the same, so we can get the maximum donations before the barrels are collected."

After a sip from her cup, she raised her brows at Jeff. "Am I forgetting anything? It sounds like you've been doing this for years."

"I think you've got it handled. Just make sure Santa is there on time."

She chuckled. "Will do. I appreciate all your help. I'll see you and Sam tonight. I'm looking forward to the parade and dinner. Is there anything I can bring?"

He shook his head. "Sam's got it covered. I'm sure you have plenty to do with the donation projects. Just come and enjoy yourself. It's always a fun evening."

She started toward the door, then stopped and lowered her voice. "One more thing. This is a personal issue. I came here for work and my own mission." She recapped her quest to find her roots. "The fire chief mentioned you might be someone to talk to about people who may have lived here at the time. I'm trying to narrow down who my mother might be."

Jeff's raised his brows. "Wow, I have a vague memory of Dad talking about a baby Chief Mercer found, but I don't remember much about it. I'll give it some thought. My mom passed away, or I'd have you visit with her. She lived on the island her whole life, as did my dad. Let me think, and I'll try to think of some old-timers that might be able to help."

"I'd appreciate it. Thanks again for your help. I'll see you later, then." She left Jeff to deal with another customer looking for a special type of hook for outdoor lights and made her way back across the street.

When she opened the door to the coffee shop, the enticing smell of cinnamon greeted her. She couldn't resist the fluffy cinnamon rolls in the case, still warm having just been delivered from the bakery.

The young woman at the counter put it in a box for her, and Noelle took her sinful breakfast upstairs and paired it with a cup of Earl Grey. As she ate a few bites, she tapped in the number for the woman at the senior center. It went to voicemail, and she left a message, asking her to call.

When she disconnected, she scanned her to-do list and checked off a few things, thanks to Jeff. She collected her purse and made her way downstairs and set out for Sweet Treats.

The woman behind the counter happily took her order for cookie trays for the two wrapping parties. When Noelle explained what they were for, the woman asked her to wait a moment and went in the back room.

After a few minutes, she returned. "I called the manager, since I know in the past, we've donated or discounted products for community events. She said she's happy to sponsor the cookie trays for you."

"That's so very kind. Thank you for doing that."

The woman assured her they would deliver the trays to the firehouse for both events and encouraged her to sample a pumpkin pie cake donut on her way out the door.

This place was growing on her.

She strolled the sidewalks, admiring the shops, decorated for the season with painted windows and lots of lights. Downtown bustled with activity and as she neared the ferry dock, the streets filled with visitors fresh from the crossing.

If the crowds were any indication, the holiday boat parade would be a most-watched event. She passed by Soup D'Jour and couldn't resist picking up a pint of their loaded baked potato soup to take home for lunch.

Smiling faces greeted her as she made her way back to the coffee shop, which was packed with people waiting to be served. She wound her way around them and up the stairs to her quiet refuge.

After stashing her soup in the fridge, Noelle glanced at her project notebook and when she put her phone on the table next to it, she noticed a text she had missed. It was from Joan, who was in the office catching up on a few things. She let her know the email went out, and she'd already received several responses from volunteers willing to help wrap.

Relieved, Noelle replied and thanked her.

She also saw a missed call from Carmen, the woman at

the senior center. She frowned at her phone, irritated she hadn't heard it ring, and pushed the button to listen to the voicemail.

Carmen invited Noelle to stop by as she was working in the office and was happy to talk more about the donation drive and party. Noelle jotted down the address and promised to see Carmen soon.

Noelle was in the habit of parking behind the hardware store and after stashing her notebook in her purse, she hurried across the street to her loaner car. The center was only a few blocks from downtown and with it being closed, she was able to park close to the side door Carmen told her to use.

It didn't take long for Carmen to show her around and explain the way they distributed gifts in the past. The large room was set up with dining tables, and Carmen expected a full house for the party and their special Christmas lunch. She also invited her to stay and join them.

Noelle got home in time for a late lunch. After the hearty soup, she curled up on the couch with a soft throw and gazed at her Christmas tree, the lights reflected in the window.

———

Almost two hours later, she woke, surprised she slept so long. Soon it would be time to meet everyone at the shop downstairs. She had time for a quick walk, though. A stroll downtown in the fresh air was exactly what she needed.

With the clouds still heavy, she opted to change into a warmer sweater and added her jacket, along with Carson's hat before heading outside. The sidewalk was filled with people, shopping and darting into eateries, while they waited for the boat parade to begin.

She wandered toward the harbor and walked along it to the marina, where a boat decked out with lights drew her attention. It was tied to the dock, with part of the lights working and part of them dark. Several boats were leaving the marina area, and she made her way closer and stepped out onto a wooden dock to get a better view.

As she gazed at the boat troubleshooting its lights and noticed a few others where the crews were making last-minute additions to the holiday decorations, she spotted a golden retriever standing at the edge of the dock. She tilted her head and studied the dog, whose tail swept across the dock in quick arcs.

"Justice, is that you?"

As soon as she uttered the words, the dog grabbed her leash and carried it, while she rushed toward Noelle and sat at her feet. Noelle petted the top of her head and scanned the area. Carson must be nearby if Justice was here.

Moments later, his deep voice came from behind her. "Hey, Noelle. I was just checking on our rescue boat to make sure it was up to snuff." He pointed at a boat in the marina.

"You aren't going to pilot it?"

He shook his head. "Nah, I'll let one of the young guns do the honors. I'd much rather enjoy the parade tonight."

She pointed at the mass of boats heading to the right of where they were standing. "So, where are they all going?"

"Oh, they stage at Shipyard Cove and then travel up here to put on the show for everyone and end up in the harbor."

"I see. I've never been to a boat parade."

"It's a tradition here on the island. Everyone loves the lights."

"I ran into Jeff. He was checking on our spot to watch the parade. One of the firemen, Steve, is setting us up at the marina in the yacht club. It's got a wonderful view."

They wandered back toward downtown, where people crowded into restaurants along the water, vying for the best views for the parade.

He tapped the brim of his hat, which resembled the one she wore, but was official with a patch from the sheriff's office. "The hat looks good on you."

She chuckled. "Well, it looked like it might decide to rain. I wasn't sure." She lowered her voice and whispered, "It also covers my gray roots showing on the crown of my head."

He chuckled. "I'm no hair expert, but Jeff's sister has a salon. I'm sure Sam or Jeff could hook you up with her." He held up his hands. "Not that you need it. Just information." He glanced up at the clouds. "I think the forecast for showers tonight might be right. Hopefully, after the parade."

He darted into the backdoor of Cooper Hardware and left Justice in Jeff's office, where he introduced Noelle to Bailey and Zoe, who belonged to Jeff and Sam. "Jeff offers free dog sitting on the side." He smiled at Justice. "You have fun with your friends, and I'll pick you up in a little while." He patted her head and left the three furry friends to play.

They crossed the street, and he held the door of the coffee shop open. The place was packed. Carson led the way to the side of the store lined with bookshelves and a few comfy chairs amid only a couple of tables. Several people were there, visiting and laughing, holding cups.

Carson stepped forward and shook the hand of a man with silvery gray hair. "Spence, how are you? I wanted to introduce everyone to Noelle. She's here visiting for the holidays and staying upstairs in Sam's apartment."

Spence smiled at Noelle and shook her hand, as did the elegant woman next to him, who introduced herself as Kate. "Lovely to meet you, Noelle. Sam told us she had a visitor staying above the shop for the holidays."

Noelle said hello to them and the others, trying to keep their names straight. Max, a doctor and his wife Linda, the florist. Dean, a photographer and his service dog, Rebel, along with Jess, a friendly woman who was a retired teacher. Izzy, a lawyer and Colin, the manager of the golf community. Blake, who was Izzy's brother and ran the local winery, and his wife Ellie. Amelia, who was spending the holidays on the island with Noah, who was an author.

Everyone was friendly and welcoming, anxious to know more about Noelle and peppering her with questions.

Sam came from around the corner with a drink tray and handed Carson his and with a wink, placed a warm cup in Noelle's hand. "Chai tea latte for you."

Jeff came through the door and hurried toward Sam. He greeted her with a quick kiss and took the mocha latte she had for him. "Okay, everyone, we're all set. I just heard from Nate, and he and Regi are staying home with Emma. She's got a touch of a cold, and they don't want to chance her getting sick."

He linked his arm in Sam's and led the way out the door and down the street to the marina. The group followed, sipping their warm drinks and chatting as they made their way to the building and up the stairs where Jeff held the door and motioned everyone inside.

Along with chairs, tables, and warmth, the room boasted huge windows that looked out on the water. Carson led Noelle to a chair and pointed out the window. "Here they come."

The first boat, a huge one with thousands of twinkling lights and even a Santa onboard came into view. More boats followed, their colorful lights reflected in the calm waters of the harbor.

The sheriff's rescue boat and the fire department's boat

sounded their sirens, and the crowd lining the waterway broke into applause. All the boats were beautiful, but Noelle was partial to the simpler sailboats outlined in lights. They were quiet and relaxing.

Along with the festive parade, the friendly group of people, who visited with her during the display, lifted her spirits. She realized how solitary her life at home really was. She spent her days at work and her evenings grading papers or preparing for lectures. The highlights of her nights at home were a new bottle of wine or a new episode of a show she enjoyed.

She rarely went out and when she did, it was always associated with her work. She ventured out to dinner by herself occasionally, but more often than not, opted to get something to go and brought it home to eat.

Over the years since Courtney left for college, Noelle spent all her free time with her beloved wheaten terrier, Winnie, or her mom. Now, with both of them gone, she was truly alone.

As she laughed at something Izzy said, she realized how much she missed not having a close circle of friends. She'd never been a huge group person and tended to shy away from social events, but this felt different. This felt genuine.

Everyone was kind and friendly. Sam and Jeff hadn't hesitated to help her, even though she was a literal stranger. The others all made her feel at home and were interested in the work she did and even more in her as a person.

As she gazed out the window at the grand finale of boats coming into view, fireworks exploded in the sky above them. She gasped. The bursts of color lit up the indigo sky and reflected in the water below. Combined with the colorful lights from the boats, it was nothing short of magical.

When the fireworks ended, Jeff reminded everyone to

come out to the house, where a feast was waiting for them. Carson offered Noelle his arm as they walked back to the hardware store. He collected Justice and waited for Noelle to run up to the apartment and grab the bottles of wine she bought to contribute to the gathering.

Once Noelle was settled in the passenger seat, he got behind the wheel. "I need to swing by the house and drop Justice off. It will only take a few minutes."

"I don't mind. I'm in no hurry."

He smiled at her. "I'll give you a quick tour, if you'd like."

"I'd love that." She rested her head against the back of the seat and sighed. She was more than a little curious to see where Carson lived.

"It's the house I grew up in. When Dad passed away, Mom moved into town, and I moved back home."

She perked up at that news. She was even more interested since she spent time there the first week of her life. She couldn't wait to see it now.

CHAPTER TEN

C arson turned off the main road. "The house is near Smuggler's Cove but not on the water. I renovated it after Mom moved out and modernized it. It's got what realtors call a filtered water view. Lots of trees on the property, and you can see the water from the deck, but you'll have to come back in the daytime to appreciate it."

He took a few turns through the heavily forested neighborhood and stopped in front of a large gate. He pressed a button on a remote in the console, and it swung open.

As soon as he parked the truck near the garage door, Justice's tail thumped against the backseat, and she pressed her nose against the window.

Noelle took in the colorful bulbs that lit up the roofline of the house and the warm glow that came from the frosted glass in the door and sidelights. He opened both passenger doors, and Justice bounded out of her seat and made a beeline for the front door. Carson unlocked the door, where a fresh wreath hung, and she bolted inside. He held it open for Noelle. "Come on in."

She walked through the door and into the open kitchen and living area. It smelled of fresh pine, like her apartment. He opened a pantry door and dished up some kibble for Justice. The golden watched his every move as he opened the fridge and added something to the top of her bowl, along with some frozen blueberries.

The minute he set the bowl on her food mat, Justice dug into her dinner. Carson gestured to the kitchen. "Feel free to look around. I'm going to change, then I'll give you a quick tour."

He took the hallway off the kitchen and left Noelle to her own devices. With her hand on the cool gray and white granite island counter, she admired the white cabinets and stainless-steel appliances. Carson kept a very tidy house.

Open to the kitchen was the living area with large glass doors and a view of the back deck and what she imagined was the filtered water view Carson described. Along with the soft lighting coming from the low deck lights along the edge of the house, twinkle lights were wrapped along the railing of the deck, giving it an inviting look. Carson's Christmas tree was in the corner of the living room, lit with white lights. She noticed the electric fireplace in the narrow wall that separated the two glass doors in the living room.

She wandered to the opposite hallway from where Carson went and found two guest bedrooms, one of which was outfitted with a desk and served as an office, and a bathroom done in coastal blue tones.

The oversized back door, with a dog door cut into the wall next to it, and a large walk-in storage area complete with deep shelves and outfitted with hooks for coats and winter gear, was at the end of the hallway.

Justice came down the hallway and exited through the flap of her door. Noelle made her way back to the kitchen atop the weathered gray wooden flooring that ran throughout the entire space. There was no dining room, but three bar-height chairs were stationed on one side of the granite island.

It was a simple and functional layout that suited Carson well. From what she remembered of the photos Betty had given her, she didn't recognize anything. The interior looked like nothing captured in the shots from fifty years ago. Carson's remodel must have been substantial.

Moments later, he returned in jeans and a gray henley shirt that accentuated his graying temples. She smiled at him. "Your home is lovely." She paused and added, "I think I recognized that chair that's in your guest room. The green one with the wooden feet. I remember that style from those photos your mom shared."

He nodded. "I'm impressed. You've got a good eye for detail. Yes, I had it reupholstered." He pointed at the kitchen. "I opened up this whole area and made it one space. Our old kitchen was really small. I'm not sure how Mom managed in it."

He motioned her to follow him. "I'll show you the master suite, then we can hit the road." She took in the space, where the gray and white theme carried over, except for a coastal blue shiplap wall behind the bed. He had a sliding glass door that led to the rear deck and a nice walk-in closet, plus a huge master bathroom.

The spacious walk-in shower dominated one side of the room and a double vanity with oversize countertop sinks and a large counter between them took up the opposite wall.

Like the rest of his home, the master suite was neat and uncluttered, with few decorations, save for a few family photos, some fish-themed wall art, photos of Justice, and a pretty bowl of polished rocks. She noted the bookcase in his bedroom, and the office was filled with a variety of fiction and nonfiction titles.

"It's very nice. So serene and peaceful. I imagine in your line of work, it's nice to have such a quiet haven."

He gestured toward the door. "It's what I love about it out here. It's peaceful and close enough to town that I can get there quickly, but far enough away to make me feel like I'm tucked away in the forest."

When they walked into the kitchen, they found Justice lounging on her bed in the corner of the living area. When he bent down to pet her, Noelle noticed the holster on his side. She'd never been around anyone in law enforcement but imagined carrying was a necessity.

He stood and met Noelle's eyes. "This year, it's just Mom and me for Christmas. We'd love it if you would join us. Nothing fancy, just here at the house. I thought you might not have plans and wanted to be sure you were invited."

Her heart warmed at the touching invitation. "I'd love to. I hadn't given Christmas much thought, but I'd love to spend it with you and your mom. Can I bring anything?"

With a shake of his head, he said, "Absolutely not. I'm making a simple brunch, then we'll have dinner in the evening. Come out whenever you like. We might put you to work in the kitchen, but Mom and I have everything covered."

"Count me in. That sounds wonderful."

He collected his jacket, promised Justice he'd be back soon, and locked the door behind them. As he circled around the driveway, his headlights illuminated another building. "That's my dad's old shop. He liked to tinker, and I still use it. Plus, the attached carport comes in handy."

The gate closed behind them and once they were on the road, it was only a few minutes before he took another turn toward the water and drove down a winding driveway.

She gasped as the huge house, lit up with Christmas lights, came into view. "Wow."

He chuckled. "Wow is right. Sam and Jeff have an awesome place here. You'll love it, and I guarantee you won't go away hungry. They've also got a nice section of beach along their property. You'll have to come again during summer."

She could definitely imagine another visit to the island.

He helped her from the truck and within a few seconds of his knock, Jeff came to the door. Soft Christmas instrumental music drifted from inside, mixed with the louder sounds of laughter and conversation.

"Come in, welcome," said Jeff. He took their coats and led the way through the huge great room with windows making up most of the back wall, where a majestic tree twinkling with white lights graced the space. A massive stone fireplace, where a fire glowed, drew her attention. The room was stunning.

They went through an opening into the kitchen, where everyone was gathered or seated around the large dining table. Jeff hurried to help Sam take a pan out of the oven.

She turned and grinned. "You two are just in time." She pointed out Max, who was handling beverages. In no time, he delivered a glass of wine to Noelle and an Arnold Palmer to Carson.

Jeff whistled, and everyone stopped talking.

"We're going casual buffet style tonight. All the food is here on the island, and we've got plates and silverware stacked. Just fill your own plate and between the dining table and the living room, we have plenty of space for everyone."

Noelle glanced over at the dining table, and Izzy waved and pointed to two empty chairs between her and Kate. Noelle and Carson set their drinks at the empty places and followed Izzy and Colin to the island. Kate and Spence stood behind them.

Kate reached for a plate and silverware. "Did you enjoy the boat parade, Noelle?"

"Very much. I told Carson I'd never been to one and loved all the lights, and the fireworks were a surprise."

She nodded. "It's always a special event. I'm so glad you could come tonight. Izzy and I were saying we need to organize lunch with you one day this coming week."

Jess was across the island, piling some of the apple cranberry green salad onto her plate. "Dean and I were visiting with Lulu and Jack this afternoon. She was on her way to the ferry. She's going to visit one of her daughters and grandkids for a week or so. Anyway, they said to be sure to invite everyone to come to their house the day after Christmas. They're throwing a birthday party for Regi." She made a point of catching Noelle's eye. "You, too, Noelle. You'll love Jack and Lulu. Jack is Dean's boss and is a realtor. They're Nate's parents, who you'll meet along with his wife Regi."

"I truly have no plans, so I'd love to come. Thank you," said Noelle, dishing up a turkey slider and some crab-studded macaroni and cheese.

Sam pointed at the macaroni dish. "Full disclosure. This is from Lou's. He makes the best, right?"

Everyone agreed and continued to fill their plates.

Noelle, her plate piled higher than she intended, carried it to her seat, and Izzy grinned at her. "I see you brought some wine tonight. May I compliment you on your excellent taste?" She chuckled and took a sip from her glass.

"I was so excited to learn your brother runs the local winery and is responsible for my new favorite."

"Sam tells me you're from Walla Walla. Home of many excellent vineyards. Our family has the Griffin Winery in Yakima, but I love reds, and Walla Walla has some of the best." She rattled off several family names Noelle recognized. "We have great relationships with those that have been in the industry for a long time like we have."

Noelle pointed at her glass. "I'm not much of an expert, but I usually indulge in a glass each night and have enjoyed those you mentioned."

"We'll send you home with some of ours." Izzy tilted her head toward Blake. "Or ship it if you're flying. Blake and Ellie can ship it."

Noelle nodded. "Yes, I'm flying so can't take much with me."

"We'll make sure you get some one way or the other."

Kate took a sip from her glass. "Spence is driving tonight, so I'm free to imbibe."

Noelle tilted her head toward Carson. "I've got a designated driver myself."

"The best kind," said Kate, with a grin. "I was serious about lunch. Do you have a day that works best for you? Are you done with your work at the school district?"

"I'm all finished. I volunteered to help Carson with the donation drive, so that's keeping me busy, but I'm sure I can squeeze in lunch. Maybe Monday?"

Izzy agreed that was perfect, since she and Blake were going to Yakima to spend Christmas with their parents and leaving on Thursday. Before Noelle knew it, Izzy was organizing a group lunch and inviting everyone to come to her house. She asked Colin to put in a catering order at the clubhouse restaurant. "They can do our main entrees, and I'll add a few side dishes." Izzy smiled at Noelle. "All set. I'll text you my address and plan to come over whenever you want Monday. We'll eat around noon."

Jess was excited it was Monday since she and Dean were flying to Maine to spend the holidays with her son on Wednesday. Even Linda, who was beyond busy with the Christmas rush at the flower shop and nursery, promised to pop in for lunch.

Kate agreed. "Monday is perfect. I'm off that day, and my son is coming to spend Christmas with us and arrives on Thursday, so that will give me time to get prepared."

Noelle finished the last bite from her plate. "I can't remember where you work, Kate."

"Oh, I own an antique and art shop downtown. You'll have to stop by when you have time."

"I'd love that. I'll make sure to visit before I leave."

Amelia leaned into Noah's shoulder. "I'm sure Noah and his son would welcome a chance to spend some time together without me. I've been sneaking off to visit my sister and her husband and would love to come to lunch."

Izzy finished her sip of wine, then held up her hand. "Oh, bring Georgia. The more the merrier."

Amelia smiled. "I'll do that. She would love the chance to visit with all of you." She turned toward Noelle. "Georgia and her husband Dale have a house just down the street from Jess and Izzy."

Max and Jeff collected the dishes, and Carson and Spence, along with Dean and Blake, volunteered to take care of them. Sam put Noah and Colin in charge of serving dessert.

While the men worked, Sam slipped into Carson's empty chair, next to Noelle. She lowered her voice. "A little bird told me you were hoping to get your hair colored."

Noelle laughed. "A bird with a badge, I bet."

Sam grinned and held up her phone. "Anyway, I texted Jen, Jeff's sister, who does my hair, and I think everyone else's. She said she's going to be in the shop tomorrow and could do you then if you can be there by ten."

"Wow," said Noelle, her eyes wide. "That would be wonderful. Carson mentioned her, but I figured this time of year would be impossible, so I resolved myself to wearing hats as much as possible."

Sam chuckled. "I know the struggle. Anyway, her shop is just down from mine on the other side of the street. I'll text you the info."

"I'll be there. Thank you so much."

Noah and Colin arrived with brownie sundaes for everyone. Jeff and Max followed with the offer of coffee and tea, and Blake added a few more bottles of wine to the table.

As Noelle savored the brownie and ice cream smothered in hot fudge sauce, she soaked in the warmth of the group of people she already thought of as friends. Like the blanket of stars in the dark sky, they provided comfort and hope. Both of which were things she'd given up on these last few months.

CHAPTER ELEVEN

After Carson walked her to her door after midnight, Noelle slept late on Sunday. Once dressed, she stopped downstairs and, along with her chai tea latte, asked the barista to make her a drink for Jen. The young woman smiled and made her a peppermint mocha latte to take with her.

With the shop technically closed, Noelle had to tap on the glass door. A woman with a wide smile and her blondish hair piled into a messy bun unlocked the door. "You must be Noelle. Come on in."

Noelle handed her the drink. "I brought you a peppermint mocha as a small thank you for squeezing me in today."

"Aww, that's so sweet. Come on over to my station, and we'll get you fixed up in no time."

Like Jeff, Jen was easy to talk to and made Noelle feel right at home. She did a fabulous job on her hair, restoring the coppery highlights and the deeper chestnut to her dull brown hair. The gray was gone, and the fresh cut and style were flattering. Noelle added a generous tip to the credit card slip and thanked Jen again before setting out for her apartment.

She spent the rest of the day lounging, reading, watching a few shows, and waiting for the soup she put in the slow cooker to finish.

As she filled the electric kettle and selected Earl Grey from her tea stash, she couldn't help but think of her mom. She would have loved the island and the holiday activities. How she wished she were with her now.

The more she dug into her past, Noelle was convinced her mother didn't know who her birth mother was or any more than she did at this point. She had so many questions and despite wanting to ask her mom, she feared she wouldn't have the answers either.

She also found herself reflecting on the wonderful evening she enjoyed at Sam's house. She was fifty years old and had never had friends like the group she met there. Granted, she wasn't outgoing. An introvert at heart, she preferred being alone, working, and the quiet that came with it. At least she thought she did.

When Tom passed away so young, Noelle shouldered all the responsibilities they'd shared on her own. She pulled herself up by her bootstraps and made a life for her young daughter. She put everything she had into having a successful and stable career. Between work and keeping up with things at home, it left little time for socializing.

Along with visiting last night, she'd managed to recruit several volunteers to help wrap presents for the donation drives. Their willingness to pitch in during the busy season, and with little notice, meant the world to Noelle.

It had been years since she'd had such a fun time visiting and being part of a group. She learned more about each of them and was still fangirling over meeting Noah, an author she read and adored. He was gracious and let her wax on about how much she enjoyed his stories.

Along with Noah, she enjoyed listening to Spence regale the group with stories from his long career as a detective in Seattle. She also couldn't get enough of Zoe and Bailey, not to mention Dean's dog, Rebel. They were all well behaved and loved the attention.

Their presence reminded Noelle how much she missed her faithful friend, Winnie. After losing her and her mother in short succession, Noelle wasn't sure she wanted another dog. The pain of loss was so intense, and she didn't want to face it again. Being around Justice and the others made her question that decision.

Winnie's absence left a definite hole in her life. Perhaps a new friend wouldn't be such a horrible idea.

After a restful Sunday, when Monday dawned, Noelle woke up happy and ready for the day, eager to spend the afternoon with the group of women she'd only just met but felt as if she'd known for years. She was even more happy when she checked her hair in the mirror and found it still looked fabulous after a night of sleeping on it.

After her morning latte from Sam's shop, she headed to the sheriff's office to check on her volunteer work. She found Joan at her desk. "Morning, Joan. How's it going?"

"Living the dream, Noelle." She smiled and reached for a file folder. "I forwarded you some emails and have a tally here on volunteers for the wrapping parties." She handed Noelle the folder. "It's looking good. Sheriff Mercer is in a meeting all morning."

She thanked Joan and took the folder to the conference room. Joan was right. Things were shaping up and based on the prior lists, she had more than enough help for the wrapping activities.

There was also a message in the file from George, the now retired but long-serving sheriff, who always volunteered to be Santa for the kids. He had it on his calendar and would be at the fire station early, in his suit, ready to greet the children.

With that good news, she checked another item off her list and put in a call to the school. She spoke with the secretary who was coordinating the students who would need transportation to the fire station for the party on Friday.

Many parents brought their children after school, but the school arranged for a bus to transport the kids whose parents worked or who couldn't otherwise take them on their own.

Noelle confirmed the time, and the secretary let her know that they would have one bus load, and it would arrive at three o'clock. They only had one teacher to chaperone, so she was hoping Noelle and the others could pitch in and help keep an eye on the children. The teacher would stay to check out the kids when their parents arrived around five o'clock.

As she scribbled a few notes, Noelle thanked her and gave the secretary her cell number in case anything came up during the event.

Noelle checked her master list again and was about to put the files away when Joan came through the door. She waved a check in the air. "We just got a nice donation from Rotary Club. They usually send along a check each year to allow us to shop for anything we're short on in the donation department."

She handed the check to Noelle. The amount was more than she expected. She looked at Joan. "I guess I better go and check on the barrels and see what we're short on so I can do some quick shopping."

She tucked the file folder under her arm and collected her purse. "I've got a lunch date, but I'll be available on my cell phone if anything comes up. Jeff's crew is collecting the toy barrels today, so I'll survey those this afternoon and visit the other locations for the seniors and figure out what we might need."

She left Joan with a wave and hurried to the parking lot.

Izzy's directions were spot on, and it didn't take long for Noelle to make the turn into the golf community. She wound her way through the streets graced with perfectly manicured lawns and planters and pulled in front of Izzy's house.

Jess answered the doorbell and welcomed Noelle with a hug. "Come in and get something to drink."

She led Noelle through the entry and into the kitchen, where Izzy was chopping fruit, and Kate was arranging plates and silverware on the dining table. Izzy looked up and smiled. "Help yourself to something to drink." She gestured to the array of wine, lemonade, and iced tea, on the large granite island counter.

Kate came from the dining room. "I've got a pitcher of iced water on the table, too." She smiled at Noelle. "Your hair looks terrific."

Noelle touched the side of her hair. "Thanks to Jen and Sam for getting me in yesterday."

Izzy slid the diced apples from the cutting board and into a bowl. "Jen is a magician. We all love her. I invited her today, but she's booked. Emma is still not feeling great, so Regi is staying home with her and won't be here. Ellie will be here but can't stay long. She's got some work to do for a Christmas party at the winery."

"That's still on my list. I have to visit before I leave," said Noelle, pouring iced tea into her glass.

Moments later, the bell rang out, and Jess rushed to answer the door. She returned with Sam and Amelia, along with her sister Georgia. Amelia introduced her to Noelle, and Georgia engulfed her in a hug. "So nice to meet you and thanks to Izzy for inviting me. This is lovely."

Linda and Ellie arrived next and on their heels came Colin, toting food to the kitchen. Izzy thanked him with a kiss and encouraged everyone to grab their plates. "Colin talked me into doing brunch, so we have a yummy eggs benedict casserole, a French toast casserole, and a huge charcuterie board with all sorts of deliciousness, courtesy of the clubhouse restaurant."

She added the winter fruit salad to the spread, and the ladies chatted while they circled the island and filled their plates.

Sam was in front of Noelle and caught Izzy's eye. "Where's Sunny?"

Izzy smiled. "She's with Colin and Jethro. They're having a playdate at his place."

Sam grinned at Noelle. "They're both beautiful goldens."

Linda laughed. "I think Ellie and I might be the only ones without a golden. I have a sweet black Labrador named Lucy."

Ellie nodded. "Yes, my Oreo is a black and white border collie. All the dogs are great friends, though."

From across the island, Jess tilted her head toward Sam. "With Dean and I heading to Maine, Sam and Jeff volunteered to watch my golden, Ruby. She'll be in heaven with their dogs."

Ellie dished up a helping of eggs benedict. "Here's to all the willing dogsitters in the group. Since we're going with Izzy to visit her parents for Christmas, Linda volunteered to take Oreo while we're away."

Linda chuckled. "Well, I volunteered Max. I'll be working until Christmas."

Ellie smiled at her. "Well, we appreciate you and Max. It's nice not to have to worry about her while we're away."

Izzy met Linda's eyes and laughed as she filled her wine glass. "Count your lucky stars Colin is staying home this year, or you'd have two more to deal with. It takes me back to days of trying to find a babysitter for my daughter."

Noelle took her plate to the dining room and ended up at the seat between Ellie and Izzy. As they ate and visited, Ellie extended an invite to Noelle and the others. "We're doing a little locals appreciation gathering after Christmas on Friday the twenty-seventh. Nothing huge, just appetizers and wine, of course. Just a little treat for our local customers and visitors."

"Oh, that sounds perfect," said Noelle. The others chimed in with their agreement, and everyone planned to be there.

"How's the donation drive going, Noelle?" asked Amelia. "I volunteer at the food bank and do the deliveries, with most of my clients being seniors. They're excited about the upcoming party."

"So far, so good. We just received a donation today, so I need to figure out what more we might need and do some quick shopping." She glanced over at Sam. "I'm going to stop by and see Jeff after I'm done here and make sure we have enough toys, too."

Amelia nodded. "Well, from what I know in visiting with so many of them, you can never have enough socks, slippers, blankets, and just basic necessities like toothpaste, paper goods, shampoo, and soap. They love anything and are always so thankful for the smallest kindness."

"Oh, that's good to know. That will help me in my shopping adventure."

Amelia refilled her water and Georgia's. "I'll be at the party on Monday to help out. Then, we deliver the gifts to those homebound seniors who can't come to the party, so we're gearing up for a big day on Tuesday."

Georgia smiled. "She even recruited me to help. I think Dale might come with me." She paused and then added, "Amelia told me about the wrapping party, and Dale and I will be there for sure on Saturday to help."

"Aww, that's wonderful. Thank you," said Noelle. "I'm really looking forward to the party on Friday for the kids."

Linda pushed her chair back from the table. "I hate to eat and run, everyone, but we're slammed at the nursery. I'll be glad when Christmas arrives, and we close it down for the season."

She hugged Izzy, thanked her for lunch, and said her goodbyes before seeing herself to the door. After she left, Izzy said, "I hope she gets some rest after Christmas. She's been working way too hard."

Sam smiled and lowered her voice. "Can you all keep a secret?"

Everyone nodded. "Max is treating Linda to a European river cruise. They leave right after Christmas for two weeks. He's worked to get the flower shop covered and has organized everything."

Izzy's eyes went wide. "He is a definite keeper. What a lovely idea."

Sam nodded. "Max has always been one of the best men I know. He loves Linda so much and has been dropping hints that she might want to cut back, especially at the nursery. It's so much physical work. He's hoping a couple of weeks away might sell her on the idea."

Kate nodded. "I hope it works. She deserves some time to enjoy life instead of always working."

Sam raised her brows at her friend. "From the woman who works almost full-time."

Kate blushed. "I've promised Spence I'm going to cut back on my days at the store in the new year. In fairness, I don't do near the physical work that Linda tackles. I couldn't, quite honestly."

Ellie rose and said, "All this talk about work reminds me I need to get back to the winery. I'm sure I'll see you at Regi's birthday party, if not before, but remember to put the winery on your calendar for the twenty-seventh. Merry Christmas to everyone I won't see."

Sam stepped toward her. "With Linda and Max leaving the day after Christmas, we'll watch Oreo, so you can pick her up from our place when you get home."

Jess helped clear the dishes and hugged Izzy before leaving so she could finish packing for her flight in the morning. Amelia and Georgia were next to leave, having stayed longer than they planned. They thanked Izzy and wished everyone Merry Christmas.

Sam and Kate volunteered to do the dishes and left Izzy and Noelle at the table. Izzy poured the splash of wine left in one of the bottles into her glass. "I had a quick meeting at City Hall today and found out the finance director is retiring at the end of June. The mayor is hoping to find someone with experience in governmental accounting, and I know you have a job, but I wanted to mention it to you in case you might be interested."

"Wow, that's so kind of you to think of me." She sighed and reached for her iced tea. "Actually, I've been giving more thought to retiring. Each time I think about it, I push the idea away, attributing it to losing my mom and being a bit lost. It feels like my life is unraveling."

Izzy put her hand on Noelle's arm. "Huge changes like that are difficult."

Sam and Kate came from the kitchen with mugs of hot tea for everyone. They slipped into their chairs. Kate glanced at Izzy. "This looks serious."

She smiled. "I was just telling Noelle the finance director is retiring and with her background and experience, I thought she might be interested."

Noelle shrugged. "She's given me something to think about. Without my mom and with my daughter set on marriage, there's really nothing left for me in Walla Walla. Just my work, and it doesn't hold the same excitement it used to."

Kate made eye contact with Izzy. "We didn't mention much about children at lunch out of deference to Amelia. She lost her daughter not too long ago, and the wound is still too fresh."

After a quick sip of tea, Kate continued, "I also lost a daughter, many years ago, and the holidays are always more difficult, but the loss isn't new, so it's easier to manage the memories. It's just a part of me now." She paused and added, "Tell us about your daughter."

Noelle took a deep breath and related the disappointment she felt, which led to guilt when Courtney broke the news at Thanksgiving that she was getting married. "I know it's selfish, but I'm having a hard time with it."

Kate nodded. "It's understandable. That's just one more thing that feels like loss to you. You mentioned you lost your dog, your mom, learned you were adopted, and now your daughter is planning her life thousands of miles away. I get it."

Noelle took another sip of tea and turned toward Izzy. "I'm going to give that job some serious thought. I'm contracted to teach through the first part of June, but as hard as it would be to leave the place I've called home for so long, this little island might tempt me."

Izzy grinned at her. "We have a lot to offer, not to mention a handsome lawman who I think has taken a shine to you."

Sam smiled and nodded. "Yes, I agree. I've never seen Carson so happy and take it from me, you can't do better than a guy who grew up on the island and dotes on his mom. Trust me, after giving up on the idea of marriage again, I found my true love right here."

CHAPTER TWELVE

After lingering over tea, Noelle, laden with the containers of leftovers Izzy insisted she take home, headed downtown to the hardware store.

She deposited the containers in the fridge before wandering across the street, where she found Jeff in the back of the store, supervising the sorting of the barrels. Tables were set up and labeled with pink signs for girls and blue for boys, along with age levels.

She perused the tables and discovered all of them piled high with items except the one for the oldest teen boys. After making some notes on her pad, she walked over to Jeff and asked his opinion on the shortfall.

"It's typical. Normally, there aren't many in that age group who show up to the party, and items for them are pricier, so we don't get near as many things for the high schoolers."

Noelle nodded. "Maybe I'll pick up some gift cards that are generic and if we don't give them out at the kids' party, we can use them for the seniors."

"That's a great idea. Sam and I usually wait to add to the pile, so we can definitely chip in and contribute some gift cards for the older kids. I've also got some nice fishing gear and winter jackets I can add to the collection."

"I'll get online and get some coming so they're here in time for the party. Is there anything else you can think of locally that might work?"

"Big Tony's is always popular with the kids, so gift cards for pizza might be well received."

With a nod, Noelle added that to her notepad. "Consider it done. I'll get to work on that aspect."

She left Jeff to continue the sorting process and set out for her shopping duties. She collected gift cards from Big Tony's and picked up several at the drugstore that would work for seniors.

With the remaining funds, she did some online shopping and ordered several gift cards that could work for either group. They would be delivered by Thursday, which was cutting it close, but she didn't have much choice.

After dropping off the local gift cards with Jeff, who was getting ready to go home for the evening, she went back to the apartment and settled in for a new episode of the mystery she'd started. Dinner was handled courtesy of Izzy.

She'd just finished one episode and dinner when her phone chimed.

Noelle smiled at Carson's name on the screen.

"Hey, Noelle. Hope I'm not disturbing you."

"Not at all. I'm just watching television."

"Joan said you came by this morning. Sorry I missed you. It's been a day of meetings. I just got home."

"That sounds exhausting. I'm not a big fan of meetings, and the educational system is rife with them."

"I wanted to let you know, you can count me in for the wrapping parties. I've got it on my calendar."

She smiled, and a twinge of excitement coursed through her. She hated to admit she was disappointed not to see Carson when she was in the office. "That's wonderful. I think we're covered on toys. I did a little extra gift card shopping today. Jeff's got everything at the store where they're sorting items."

"Sounds like you've got everything organized." He paused and said, "I was hoping to see you because I wanted to invite you to dinner for your birthday."

Her heart fluttered in her chest. "Aww, that's so kind of you. You really don't need to do that."

He chuckled. "I know I don't have to. I want to. I think a celebratory birthday dinner is in order to mark fifty years. Especially since you've come all this way on a quest to find out how you came to be on our tiny island. Not to mention, I enjoy spending time with you."

"Those are some compelling reasons." She laughed and said, "I'd love to go to dinner."

"I was hoping you'd say yes. I already made reservations at The Bluff. It's our newest venue overlooking the harbor."

"That sounds perfect." She would have to go shopping to find something to wear.

"I know the wrapping party is Saturday afternoon, but I made reservations for seven o'clock, thinking we'd be wrapped up by then." He chuckled.

"I see what you did there."

"I'm nothing if not clever." He cleared his throat. "Now that your birthday is settled, I have one more invite for you. Do you have any plans for New Year's Eve? The fire department has a New Year's Eve dance each year. It's always fun, and I was hoping you might go."

Sweat formed at the back of Noelle's neck. "I'm not a dancer."

"Not everyone dances. There's food, visiting, and a little dancing. The whole town is there. The best news is this year's theme is country western, so no fancy attire is required. Jeans, boots, cowboy hats, you get the idea. I heard a rumor the firefighters are making chili."

"Well, I don't have any plans, but I'm not much of a party person or a dancing person. I do like the casual dress idea, though."

"It will be lots of line dancing, which is easier than anything else. Think about it. I just wanted to get on your calendar before it filled up."

She grinned and laughed. "No chance of that. I'm hoping I have more information about my early days by then. I fly home on the third."

"I hope you have answers by then, too, Noelle."

She had no reason to think too hard. It was either the party where everyone she knew would be or sit at home in the apartment. "New Year's Eve sounds fun. I don't have any cowboy boots but count me in."

"Wonderful. You'll have fun. I guarantee it." The happy tone in his voice made Noelle smile.

"I better go," he said. "Justice is giving me the evil eye and staring at her dinner bowl."

"You two have a good night. I'll see you Wednesday if not before. Thanks again for the invitations. Both of them."

"Sweet dreams, Noelle."

She disconnected and held the phone to her chest for a few seconds. She hadn't felt that flicker of excitement since she and Tom were dating decades ago. There was definitely a spark of something between them.

She put her phone on the charger and settled back under

a blanket on the couch. It was silly to even consider something with Carson. She was leaving in ten days. Not to mention she was fifty years old and hadn't dated a man in decades.

———

Tuesday, Noelle checked in with Bunny at the historical society. She hadn't heard anything back from her inquiry with the hospital in Bellingham but promised she would call Noelle the moment she did. She suspected it might be after the holidays, though.

Sam even offered to help and sent an email to the previous owner of the coffee shop, a woman named Bea. She'd lived on the island for years, and Sam thought she might have an idea about Noelle's birth mother.

When Noelle went downstairs to get a chai tea latte, she found Sam at the register. She took her order and said, "Bea replied and said she remembered the baby being left at the fire station but didn't have a clue as to who the mother might be. She said there was a bit of chatter about it at the time, but most people thought it was someone who didn't live on the island. Seems nobody remembered anyone expecting at the time."

Noelle thanked her and shuffled to a table. The realization that she may never get her answers weighed on her.

As she sipped and pondered, Amelia and Georgia came through the door. They smiled and asked if they could join her.

Happy for the company and the distraction, Noelle welcomed them. When they returned, Amelia caught her eye. "I've got to run to my volunteer job in a few minutes, but I'm so happy we ran into you. We wondered if you had plans for Christmas Eve?"

With a shake of her head, Noelle smiled. "No, no plans."

Amelia grinned at her sister. "We'd love to have you join us. We're gathering at Noah's house. His son is here visiting, and Georgia has some of her family coming from Lavender Valley. It's just casual. We're doing appetizers, games, movies. Nothing fancy."

Her heart filled with warmth, Noelle nodded. "I'd love to come. It's so nice of you to offer." She took a sip from her cup. "I'm just blown away by all of you. Everyone has been so kind and friendly. It's quite lovely." Tears burned in her eyes as her voice cracked.

Georgia reached across the table and patted her hand. "That's just one reason I love it here so much. I can't wait to introduce you to some of my family. I call them my sisters of the heart because we were all foster children raised by the same wonderful parents in Oregon. Believe me, I understand what it's like to be alone, especially during the holidays, and we'd like nothing more than for you to spend yours with us."

Amelia nodded. "I'll text you the address. Come out any time after four o'clock and if you want to bring an appetizer or dessert to share, feel free, but don't stress about it. We'll have plenty."

"I look forward to it. Thank you again for making me feel so welcome."

Before they left, both of them waved goodbye and promised to see her at the wrapping party tomorrow.

As Noelle added the event to her calendar on her phone, she chuckled. She had more of a social life on the island after ten days than she had in years of living in Walla Walla. As she eyed the calendar, the birthday dinner stood out.

She finished her drink and set out in search of something

new to wear for her birthday date. That was a word she hadn't thought of in a very long time. A word she never expected to use.

She wandered down the street and saw Kate through the window of her shop. Noelle opened the door and waited for her to finish with a customer. While she waited, she wandered through the shop, admiring the beautiful furniture and artwork.

Moments later, Kate touched her shoulder. "Well, hello, Noelle. Lovely to see you. I'm so glad you stopped in."

"Your shop is gorgeous. I can see why everyone envies your decorating talents."

Kate blushed and waved away the praise. "Oh, it's just what I enjoy doing. My hobby turned into a business years ago, and I can't seem to let it go. I truly enjoy it."

As Noelle went from display to display, admiring the beautiful table settings atop the wood dining room sets and the deep colors Kate used in the furnishings for a masculine home office, Noelle pointed at Kate's stylish poncho. "That's so cute. I'm actually on a quest to find something to wear to dinner. Carson invited me to The Bluff for my birthday, and I don't have much between jeans and suits with me."

Kate glanced at the sleeve of her poncho. "I got this here. There's a cute little boutique at the end of the street. It's called Island Chic. She carries lots of unique items, and her prices are great."

"Thanks for the tip. I'll head that way."

With one last gaze around the space, Noelle smiled. "I would be embarrassed if you ever came to my house and saw all my white walls, with barely any décor, and definitely not a theme, like all these lovely rooms you've showcased here."

With a wink, Kate grinned. "White walls are my favorite. It's a blank canvas that gives me total freedom."

"Izzy told me you helped her with her place, and it's perfect. I love all those coastal colors. They're so relaxing."

"The one I had the most fun with this year was Noah's. He bought a place and asked me to help him decorate. He gave me free rein, with Amelia, of course. She visits and stays with him often. He also goes over to Driftwood Bay and visits her."

"They're making a long-distance relationship work, huh?"

Kate nodded. "They seem to be. It's relatively new, and Noah needs space and time to write, so I think it suits them. Amelia owns a bookstore and, from what I know, plans to be there for busy times and spend the slower times here."

"Sounds like a perfect match." Noelle gestured to the door. "Thanks for the tip on the boutique. I'll see you tomorrow."

Kate waved goodbye and greeted the two new customers who came through the door with a warm smile.

Noelle set off in the direction Kate told her and, had she not been looking for the store, would have missed it. It was around the curve of the street and in a little old house that didn't look like a retail space.

She stepped through the blue door, and a dark-haired women with a friendly smile greeted her. "Welcome in." She pointed out the different rooms in the house and let Noelle know about the sale room near the back. "Feel free to browse and if you need help with anything, just let me know. I'm Deb."

Noelle thanked her and headed to the sale room. She was nothing if not frugal.

She ignored the rack of dresses and looked at the selection of pants and shirts. She was on her second pass through them when Deb came through the door. "Are you looking for something special?"

Noelle sighed. "I'm going to a birthday dinner and wanted something dressier than what I brought with me, but nothing over the top." She pointed at a pair of jeans. "I'm also going to the New Year's Eve party and could use something to pair with jeans."

Deb nodded. "I have some ideas." She stepped over to the rack of dresses and when she met Noelle's eyes, she grinned. "Humor me. Just try this one."

Before Noelle knew it, Deb had her settled in a dressing room with several garments hanging on the hooks, awaiting her judgment.

With great reluctance, she slipped the soft sweaterdress over her head. It had a subtle cowl neck. The deep copper color picked up the highlights in her hair. Noelle turned to check it in the mirror and couldn't find anything negative to say. It fit perfectly, and she had a pair of leather dress boots she brought with her that would work with it.

Deb knocked on the door. "Here's one more thing to try. I think you could wear it with a pretty blouse for the New Year's Eve party."

Noelle opened the door, and Deb's smile widened. "That looks fabulous. Let me get you a belt, and it will look even better." She handed Noelle the black suede and leather jacket and a gray shirt with subtle glittery sparkles in the fabric.

While she waited for the belt, Noelle held up the shirt and jacket with a pair of sale jeans. It was a cute outfit. One that she hoped fit.

An hour later, Noelle left the store with both outfits, including a new pair of jeans. Everything but the jacket was on sale, and Deb was kind enough to give her a discount on it. She spent more than she planned but justified it when she remembered she hadn't bought any new clothes for the last two years.

On her way back to the apartment, she detoured to Dottie's Deli and picked up a sandwich and salad to go.

After she put her new wardrobe in the closet, Noelle put in a call to the bakery to double-check the cookie tray delivery for the wrapping parties. They confirmed the times, and Noelle disconnected and plated her very late lunch.

Before she settled in to watch the mystery series she enjoyed, Noelle took one more look at her project checklist. She called the fire chief to make sure he was ready for the wrapping party tomorrow and promised to be there early to help set up the room.

She resisted the urge to ask if he'd thought of anyone else who might have a clue that would help her locate her birth mother. She'd wait and ask him in person. She closed the project folder and sighed. Everything was handled. It should be smooth sailing and by Monday, her duties would be complete.

CHAPTER THIRTEEN

O nce Noelle confirmed Jeff's crew delivered the barrels of toys to the fire station, she headed over to get things organized. Armed with her list of gift wrap Jeff was providing, she set up a system that would make their process foolproof when it came to dispersing the gifts.

Along with the labels on the barrels, each age group would use a specific paper, as well as different wraps for the boys and girls. That way, if anything got jumbled, Noelle could tell who the toy was destined for with a quick glance.

The fire chief had tables and chairs set up, and Noelle spent the afternoon getting each table outfitted with supplies and set up an assembly line of sorts for wrapping and ribbons. She slid two empty barrels, one for boys and the other for girls, at the end of each table, labeled with the toy categories.

One of the firefighters passed through and, while he was there, showed Noelle where she could find the supplies for the beverages. He toted the huge coffee pots over, and she went about setting up tea and cocoa packets, along with paper cups and lids. She made sure to leave room for the cookie trays, which arrived while she was adding holiday napkins to the table.

With everything situated, Noelle wrapped a sample toy at each table, so those working would have a visual of the paper for the girls and the one for the boys. Once her samples were done, she set herself up next to the bin with the most toys and wrapped them.

It wasn't long before her volunteers arrived. She greeted each of them at the door and thanked them, happy to see Kate, Amelia, Georgia, Izzy, and Sam come through the door. Georgia introduced her to her husband Dale, who was in line for cookies.

After several women who said they were married to some of the firefighters arrived, Carson and Betty came through the door. Betty clasped Noelle's hands in hers. "I've only got one more from the church group coming tonight. Most of us don't like driving in the dark, but we'll be here on Saturday afternoon for sure."

"That's wonderful. Not a problem. We have lots of help today."

Betty wandered over to a table, and Carson stayed behind. As soon as Noelle lined up the next group of volunteers, he motioned her toward the corner of the room. "We just had a call for the ambulance right before I picked up Mom. It was for George. Your Santa. He fell off the ladder and broke his arm."

"Oh, no. Poor guy."

Carson gritted his teeth. "I hate to be the bearer of bad news, but we're going to have to find another Santa. George has the suit, and I can go by and pick it up. He said to tell you he was sorry."

Noelle swallowed the lump in her throat. Where would she find a Santa in less than two days?

More volunteers arrived, and she nodded at Carson. "I'll get it on right away. Thanks for letting me know."

Within a few minutes, all the tables were filled with volunteers and after welcoming them again and pointing out the cookies and drinks, Noelle explained the process with the assigned wrapping papers and demonstrated how one side of the table would wrap toys for boys and the other for girls, as that would keep the assembly line flowing smoothly until the toys were deposited in the collection barrels.

The volunteers got to work, and the room was abuzz with conversation and activity. Noelle smiled and chatted with each table as she monitored things, but her mind was on Santa. Actually, the lack of one.

She scooted an empty chair up to the end of the table next to Kate, where she and the others were busy wrapping. While she loaned Kate her finger for holding the ribbon as she tied a bow, Noelle sighed.

Kate looked up and frowned. "What's wrong?"

Noelle lowered her voice. "I just found out Santa fell off a ladder and broke his arm. Now, I need to find a new one. Like fast."

Kate's eyes widened. "That's not good news at all."

"Yeah. I was feeling pretty accomplished, having everything done and ready."

Kate turned to her and raised her brows. "I happen to know a guy of a certain age with sparkling blue eyes who isn't currently employed. He'll need some extra padding, but I think he could pull it off."

Noelle reached over and gripped Kate's arm. "Do you think Spence would do it?"

"I think he would. He loves Christmas."

"Oh, that would be fantastic. I was sitting here thinking who I could ask who might be willing. I hate to interfere with your son's visit and your plans. I'm sure Jeff would do it, but he's already done so much."

Kate shook her head. "It's just a few hours, and we don't have any big plans for Friday. I'm sure he'd be open to the idea."

As she whispered to Kate, Carson came up behind her. "I've got a call and need to run. I'll make sure to pick up that suit we discussed and bring to my office. Do you think you could run my mom home if I'm not back soon?"

"Sure, I'm happy to."

He smiled. "Talk to you later?"

Her stomach did a little flip. He had a great smile. The kind that made her knees weak. "Yes, I'll call you later tonight. Thanks for helping, and I'll make sure your mom gets home safely."

He winked at her and hurried to the door.

Kate raised her brows at Noelle. "So, you and Carson seem to be hitting it off?"

With the color rising on her cheeks, Noelle smiled. "We've been spending lots of time together. He's a nice guy."

"I think that's wonderful. He's one of our favorite native islanders. He's always kind and helpful. A real pillar of the community, too." She lowered her voice. "Not to mention handsome and available."

Noelle chuckled. "I've noticed."

As they continued wrapping, Noelle's thoughts drifted to the job Izzy mentioned. She let herself imagine a new life, working on the island, having friends like Kate and Sam to call on, and just maybe a second chance at love.

With so many volunteers, it didn't take long to finish the

job and within two hours, everything was done and organized for the party. The refreshment table was neat and clean, and the leftover cookies were awaiting the firefighters who would arrive tomorrow and find a sweet treat or two.

Betty waited with Noelle, while she stood at the door and thanked all the volunteers, many of whom promised to return for Saturday afternoon. One of the firemen stayed behind to lock up, and Noelle led Betty to the car.

As Noelle started the ignition, Betty turned to her. "I'm so glad you came to the island. It's been wonderful to have you here and see you all grown up."

She put the car in gear and steered onto the street. "That's so sweet of you. I wasn't sure I should come, but I think it's the best decision I ever made. Everyone has been so kind and made me feel right at home."

"Carson mentioned you have a daughter."

With a nod, Noelle slowed as she entered town. "Yes, Courtney. She's in college and at Thanksgiving, she told me she and her fiancé are getting married. She's spending Christmas with him and his family. They have a vacation home in Vermont."

"Wow, that's exciting."

Noelle shrugged. "That's one word. I'm not as excited as I should be. I'm finding it difficult to imagine her gone for good. I had a rough time when she went to college so far away, but I always consoled myself with the idea she'd be back."

"Motherhood isn't for sissies, is it, dear?"

"No, it's not. It's just one more thing to add to my year of changes. Time goes by way too fast."

"That it does," said Betty. "It seems like just yesterday, my kids were little. You work hard to raise them to be independent and make good decisions, then in a blink of an eye, they're gone."

"I think it's lovely that Carson is still here on the island."

"Yes, it is. I'd be lost without him. He's such a good son. A good man. I'm very proud of him and thankful he's here to watch out for me. His dad would be proud of him, too."

Noelle pulled in front of Betty's cottage and hurried to open the passenger door for her. They walked to the front door where the porch light illuminated the entry. As Betty put her key in the lock, she turned to Noelle. "I meant to mention, I've been talking to all my friends who still live on the island, to see if they might remember anything that would help you figure out your birth mother. None of them remember anyone being pregnant at the time you were born. I'm afraid we've come up empty."

The sad look in Betty's eyes spoke volumes. Noelle put her hand on her shoulder. "It's okay. I'm hoping Bunny's contact at the hospital in Bellingham comes through. So far, I haven't gotten any leads. The fire chief didn't come up with anyone else I could talk to either."

Betty shook her head. "I'm so sorry, Noelle. I know how important this is to you." She stepped over the threshold. "Would you like to come in for some tea?"

As much as she would have enjoyed it, Noelle glanced back at the car. "I'm pretty tired. I think I'm just going back to the apartment and go to bed. It's been a long day."

"I understand, dear. Thank you again for the ride."

As Noelle turned to leave, Betty called out to her, "I just want you to know, your mother would be very proud of the lovely woman you've become. Even if you don't get your answers, know that she did the best she could for you. I'm sure she had every reason to believe she was giving you a better life by leaving you at the firehouse. I can't imagine how you feel, but I'm very glad we found you that day, and I'm thrilled to see you now, so beautiful and accomplished."

Tears glinted in Betty's eyes, and Noelle reached out and hugged her. By the time she released her grip on the petite woman, her own cheeks were wet. She didn't trust her voice but whispered to Betty instead, "I'm thankful you found me, too. Even if I don't find the answers here, I've found you and Carson, which is the best gift I never expected."

After making sure Betty locked her door, Noelle slid behind the wheel and drove downtown. Tears blurred her eyes as she parked in front of the shop. It was still open but not very busy. She darted inside and up the stairs before anyone caught sight of her.

She couldn't face someone asking her if she was okay or what was wrong. The sobs were at the edge of her throat and would escape at the slightest provocation.

As she entered the quiet apartment with the festive tree glowing in the window, the first sob broke free, followed by several more. She longed for her mother. Hugging Betty and listening to her wise words made Noelle realize how very much she missed her mom and the way she could make everything seem okay, no matter how big the problem.

Noelle thought she'd prepared herself for the disappointment of not finding her birth mother. Thought she was strong enough. She curled into the sofa and under the soft throw. Without thinking, she reached for her dog, who was always there to comfort her in times of sorrow.

When she found nothing but a pillow, another sob escaped. As she wiped her face and eyes, her cell phone chimed.

She tapped the screen and through a blur of tears, saw a message from Carson. *Thank you for getting Mom home. I know you're busy but hope to see you tomorrow. Sweet dreams.*

Noelle couldn't bring herself to have a conversation and replied with a happy face emoji.

The stress and emotions of the day took their toll and like a heavy weight, exhaustion settled over her as she stared at the lights on the tree until her eyes finally closed.

CHAPTER FOURTEEN

B y Friday, everything was settled, and Santa would be at the party. Spence, with Kate's help, made the suit and white beard work, and they promised to be at the fire station early so he could get in position before the children arrived.

After a quick lunch at Soup D'Jour, Noelle went to the firehouse and was on hand to supervise the moving of the barrels into position behind a makeshift curtain next to Santa's velvet chair.

As the bakery and the deli dropped off trays loaded with cookies and kid friendly mini-sandwiches, several firefighters in elf costumes came down the stairs. Soon after, Santa arrived with Kate, who helped him adjust his costume until it looked perfect.

Noelle hugged Spence, who even had little round glasses perched on his nose and looked terrific. "Thank you so much for being here, Santa." She winked at him.

"My pleasure." He made Noelle giggle when he added, "Ho-Ho-Ho."

Noelle reviewed the process with Santa and his elf helpers

and showed them the labeled barrels and the wrapping paper system. One of the elves had a camera around his neck and would be taking photos for anyone who wanted them. The others were on hand to keep the line orderly and get the age of the children as they approached Santa, so the elves behind the curtain could retrieve the appropriate toy.

With one last look at the barrels, Noelle hoped they had enough gifts for everyone who came. It was hard to predict, but based on the rough numbers the school provided and adding in the children who were homeschooled and might show up, they should be set.

She double-checked the refreshments and found several firefighters ready to serve the little ones with tables and chairs set out and plenty of treats and drinks ready for their guests.

As she walked back to the large garage area where Santa was waiting, the hiss of air brakes caught her attention. The yellow school bus pulled up in front of the bay doors.

Noelle hurried outside to meet the teacher, Miss Webb, who had a clipboard with her. The laughter and giggles from the bus floated through the open door. The kids were excited and itching to get their time with Santa.

Miss Webb ran a tight ship and directed the children off the bus in an orderly fashion, checking off their names as they exited. She made a point of telling Noelle that anyone who showed up to collect the children after the event had to check with her and sign them out.

Noelle promised to let everyone know the rule and helped lead the kids into the multi-purpose room for refreshments. The firefighters were on hand to show them the restrooms and get them situated at the tables.

Soon after the bus arrived, more and more children,

accompanied by their parents, came through the door and filtered into the room to get their refreshments. With the room filled, one of Santa's elves came to the door to escort the first table to Santa.

Noelle followed them out to observe. Spence looked perfect sitting on the velvet chair, and the kids were excited to see him and collect their gifts. So far, so good. She just had to get through the next couple of hours.

After the first hour, they gave Santa a break, and Miss Webb led the kids in a few Christmas carols while they continued to snack and drink cocoa. After thanking the firefighters, several of the children who already received a gift and came with their parents left the party.

Once Spence was back in the chair, the process continued. It warmed Noelle's heart to see the happy smiles and excited faces of the kids with their gifts. The giggles and gasps made all the work worth it.

By five fifteen, all but about half of the children who arrived on the bus had been picked up by their parents. Santa's work was done, and he and Kate slipped out the back door so as not to chance ruining the illusion for any of the children.

Noelle was cleaning up spilled cocoa at one of the tables when Carson came through the door and grabbed a cookie from the tray. He made his way to her and raised his brows. "Looks like it was a success."

She nodded. "Yeah, I think everyone had a good time. Santa just left. We've got a few gifts leftover, and we just need to wait until the rest of the kids are picked up, then we're done."

"I can take the leftover toys back to the office. We'll keep them in case anyone missed out today."

"Great, that would be a big help. Jeff will be by in a few minutes to pick up the empty barrels."

Carson grabbed another cookie and headed out to the main part of the firehouse.

A few minutes later, a woman came through the door and approached Miss Webb. She checked her clipboard and called out, "Jacob Malloy."

None of the kids came forward, and she called the name again. She stepped forward to a group of boys. "Have any of you seen Jacob?"

One little boy said, "He was here earlier. I think he went to the bathroom." He pointed at a chair toward the end of the table where a half cup of cocoa sat next to a plate littered with cookie crumbs.

One of the firemen offered to check the restroom. A few minutes later, he came back, shaking his head. "He's not in there, and I double checked the area around Santa's chair."

Carson came through the door, and Noelle caught his eye. "A little boy is missing. He came on the bus, and his mom is here, but we can't find him."

He stepped forward to talk to the teacher and Mrs. Malloy. Noelle stayed with the small group of kids still waiting on their parents and tried to distract them by asking about their gifts.

Soon, the rest of the parents arrived, and all the kids except Jacob were checked off the list. Miss Webb's face was filled with panic. She had her phone out to notify the principal.

Mrs. Malloy's face was etched with fear, and tears filled her eyes. Noelle brought her a cup of tea, and Carson sat with her at the table furthest from the door. He got out his notepad and asked her some questions.

The firefighters were already searching the entire building and the grounds outside, looking for Jacob. Jeff arrived, and Noelle filled him in on the missing boy. He volunteered to help search for him. He called other firemen to help.

After several minutes, Carson rose from his chair and patted Mrs. Malloy on the shoulder. "We'll start a search party right now and get you a ride home. You can wait there in case Jacob shows up at the house. If he does, just call the sheriff's office to let them know. If we find him, we'll call you right away."

One of his deputies came through the door and ushered Mrs. Malloy to his patrol unit.

Carson glanced over at Miss Webb. He asked her a few questions about Jacob and what he liked to do and if he'd been acting different at school today. She didn't have much information but was shaken up and volunteered to stay at the firehouse in case he came back there. One of the firemen in an elf costume offered to stay with her.

Carson gestured to Noelle and Jeff, and they followed him to his truck. Carson pulled a map with colored areas on it from his truck and gave it to Jeff. "The fire chief is checking the camera footage from the building. Jacob's mom said he loves boats, and he and his dad liked to go to the marina. If you can concentrate on that area and call me if you find anything, that would be great. I've got the deputies searching a two-mile radius from the fire station. I don't think he could have walked further than that in this short time, but the marina and harbor are well within that distance. Our patrol boat is also searching, and we've got deputies at the ferry terminal."

Jeff nodded his understanding and promised to keep in touch with updates.

Carson glanced over at Noelle. "Do you want to ride with me? We can take a section and work it."

"Of course. This is horrible." She climbed into the passenger seat and listened to the voices on the radio. She only caught a few words. They were hard to understand, but Carson had no trouble and spoke into the microphone several times as they pulled away from the fire station.

As he drove, he rattled off Jacob's description. "Jacob Malloy is eight years old, wearing jeans, blue tennis shoes, a green sweatshirt, and a blue jacket. He's got brown hair and brown eyes. His mom confirmed he does not have a cell phone or any type of wearable that we could use to track him."

Noelle clutched her stomach. "This makes me sick, Carson. I can't believe I lost a kid. I'll never forgive myself it anything happens to him."

He reached across the console and took her hand in his. "We'll find him. Chances are he wandered off and got distracted or lost."

"His poor mom."

"She said his dad is in the military and was going to be home for Christmas, but they just got word last night that he can't come. Jacob was really disappointed and upset about it."

Tears leaked from Noelle's eyes. "Aww, poor little guy."

Carson drove through the streets at a slow pace, with each of them scanning the sidewalks for movement.

Every few minutes, a voice on the radio came through to report their progress at various sections throughout the areas within the radius. Two miles didn't sound like much, but it was a large swath of downtown and if Jacob headed the opposite direction, more into the rural area, he might be even harder to find.

Noelle tried not to think the worst and keep her eyes

peeled for Jacob. "At least the Christmas lights help illuminate the streets. It makes it easier to distinguish movement."

Carson nodded as he scanned his side of the street. "His mom said Jacob loves Christmas and the lights and the tree downtown. We swept that area but didn't find him. We should focus on decorated and lit places. If he likes that, he might be drawn to those spots."

"Good idea. Most of downtown is decorated. What about his school?"

Carson nodded. "We checked there first thinking he might have forgotten something and gone back instead of saying anything. Deputies checked and didn't find him there. The principal and custodians are staying at the school in case he shows up, and they're also searching the grounds."

After an hour and no sightings, Carson reported the progress to dispatch. He asked the dispatcher to activate the town emergency phone tree. When he replaced the handheld microphone, he explained to Noelle that they had a phone tree established that would alert almost all the residents of the situation and get everyone looking for Jacob.

He leaned his head against the back of the seat. "That will get lots of people checking their own yards and out looking for him. I thought we'd find him quickly, but it's getting later and later."

He pulled over and tapped his cell phone. Noelle listened for a few minutes as he received a status update from the sergeant at the sheriff's office who was keeping track of the maps and search teams.

Noelle clicked on the light above her seat and studied the map. She wasn't familiar with much but the downtown area. When she visited the senior center, she remembered seeing a park not too far away and wondered if Jacob might be drawn to one of them.

As a mom, she couldn't imagine what Mrs. Malloy was feeling. Her thoughts drifted to Courtney, who was only three when Tom died. It was a horrific time in her life, and, as she grieved, she tried to console Courtney and make the world right for her. It was impossible. She was a daddy's girl and missed him so much.

She liked to go to all the places they enjoyed together and snuggle in his sweatshirt. Anything to remind her of him.

Carson disconnected and sighed. "No sign of him yet. The fire chief checked the camera footage for us from the outdoor cameras they have on the building and found where Jacob slipped out the back door. He headed toward town. He left only about fifteen minutes before the teacher noticed he wasn't there. No ferries left during that time, so that's good news."

He tapped his phone again. "Jeff sent a text update and said no sign of Jacob at the marina. They've been going boat to boat to check all the slips, and Steve has his boat out looking along the harbor."

"I was thinking about when my husband died. Courtney was younger than Jacob. She wanted to go everywhere that reminded her of him. I wonder if there are other places besides the marina that he and his dad visited. The park, the library?"

"Good points. Let me call my deputy who's with Mrs. Malloy."

After a short conversation, Carson disconnected. "The mom says he loved going to the alpaca farm, but that's way too far away. He did visit the library, but not with his dad, and they liked to play ball at the park."

He called the sergeant tracking the search and directed

him to check those areas again. He turned to Noelle. "It makes sense that he'd go to a place he knows. Like the school, library, park, somewhere he's comfortable."

"Where does Mrs. Malloy work?"

"The dentist office on Spring Street." He put the truck in gear. They weren't too far from that, and it was in their section.

He pulled into the parking lot, and they both got out to check the area around the building, filled with grassy areas and bushes tucked into planters. Christmas lights decorated the windows, making it inviting.

They hollered out Jacob's name as they searched the area. Carson bent over and examined something on the ground. Noelle hurried to him and stared at the cellophane wrapper with a broken piece of candy cane in it. It matched the candy canes the elves were giving out to the kids after they visited with Santa.

She glanced over at Carson. "What do you think?"

"I'm hoping that means Jacob was here and dropped this. That means he might be close by. It could also mean nothing since those are generic and popular this time of year."

Finding nothing more, they climbed back into the truck and turned at the next block to finish their section of the map.

After thirty minutes of checking the sidewalks and all the side streets, Carson parked and called into the office again.

Noelle opened her door and climbed out of the truck. She stood on the corner, looking down Spring Street toward the harbor. Lots of lights twinkled in the darkness. She imagined an eight-year-old and the lure of those lights.

A few minutes later, Carson joined her. "Nothing yet, and we've swept all the sections. We only have one registered sex offender here, and deputies have already paid him a visit. His whereabouts have been verified, so that's good news. The deputy with Mrs. Malloy has contacted all of Jacob's classmates and friends and has come up empty."

Noelle pointed toward town. "I was just standing here trying to think like Jacob. I think we should walk toward town and see what catches our eye. Pretend we're eight and look for something that would attract us."

Carson made sure his handheld radio was on and let dispatch know his location and that he was on foot, searching. He collected two flashlights from the backseat and gave Noelle one. They set out in the direction of the lights of downtown filled with worry and the hope of finding Jacob.

CHAPTER FIFTEEN

Noelle pointed at a roofline of a house decorated with colorful lights and turned at the side street. Carson tilted his head toward the house. "That's a bed and breakfast."

As they came upon it, Noelle smiled. The entire front was wrapped in lights with several blowup Christmas decorations scattered in the yard. It would be a huge attraction for an eight-year-old. They both yelled out for Jacob, and Carson climbed the steps to check in with the owner.

Noelle ventured down the side of the yard, calling out as she neared the back fence.

Soon, Carson came up behind her. "The owner got the call from the telephone tree and has searched everywhere. No sign of Jacob."

"It looked so promising." Noelle trudged back toward the sidewalk, and they returned to Spring Street.

After another half block, they came to a church. As Noelle glanced over, she noticed movement in front of it. She pointed, and Carson rushed toward the entrance.

When she caught up to him, two alpacas and a donkey came into view. There was a sign advertising a live nativity that would start tomorrow and run through Christmas. The alpaca and donkeys were in a makeshift corral, awaiting their debut performance.

At the moment, they were most concerned with munching on the mounds of hay at their feet. Noelle couldn't resist getting a closer look and the opportunity to pet them if they'd let her.

Carson checked the perimeter of the church building and the planters along the front and sides of it. He came back to join Noelle and found her at the edge of the gate where all three animals were lined up, anxious for the attention.

Carson cleared his throat. "Mrs. Malloy said Jacob liked alpacas. I didn't know these were in town. They must have brought them in tonight for tomorrow's performance."

He petted the donkey and the closest alpaca and then pointed behind them. "There's a manger set up in the back."

He climbed on the rungs of the gate and jumped over it. The curious animals followed him.

As Noelle waited by the gate, her heart pounded. She closed her eyes and prayed for a miracle.

Moments later, Carson's excited shouts echoed from behind the animals. "He's here. Jacob's in the manger."

Noelle bounced from foot to foot, anxious to see the little boy.

A few minutes later, Carson emerged, his hand holding that of a little boy in jeans and blue coat. When they reached the gate, Carson picked him up and handed him over to Noelle, who hugged him close before setting him on the ground. "My name is Noelle. I'm helping Sheriff Mercer tonight. We're so glad to see you, Jacob. We're going to take you to your mommy."

Tears fell from his eyes, and he clutched Noelle's leg. With a thud, Carson vaulted over the top of the gate and landed next to them. He clicked the microphone on his shoulder and reported that Jacob had been found, and he would be transporting him to the hospital to get him checked.

The dispatcher advised the deputy with Mrs. Malloy was enroute, and they would meet Sheriff Mercer at the hospital.

Noelle bent down and kept hold of Jacob's hand. "Are you hurt? How are you feeling?"

He shook his head. "I'm just hungry. I'm not hurt."

"That's good news. We'll get you some food. Your mom is going to meet us at the hospital so the doctor can make sure you're okay. Did you fall or get hurt?"

He shook his head. "I want my mommy."

Noelle couldn't resist picking him up, and he wrapped his legs around her back and clung to her. Carson jogged ahead and promised to return with his truck.

While they waited, Noelle rocked back and forth gently, with Jacob's head tucked against her neck. Tears leaked from her eyes as she swayed with him. She whispered her thanks for his safe return and kept a tight hold on him.

Carson pulled to the curb, where Noelle was waiting, and he tried to coax Jacob away from her, but he wasn't having it. She suggested she climb into the backseat, and Jacob could sit on her lap while Carson drove.

Jacob agreed to let Carson hold him while she did and when Carson placed him in the back with her, he cuddled against her. It didn't take long for Carson to get to the hospital, where several sheriff vehicles were already at the emergency room entrance.

As soon as Carson opened the back door of his truck,

Mrs. Malloy rushed toward it. Jacob bounded off Noelle's lap and into his mother's arms.

She held him close, tears flowing, as she whispered in his ear. Carson stepped over to her. "We'll just have the doc check him out to make sure he's in good shape, then we'll take you both home."

"Thank you, Sheriff Mercer. Thank you so much for finding him."

"It was a group effort." He glanced over at Noelle. "Ms. Davis suggested we walk toward town and pretend we were eight years old, looking for things that might be interesting. We found him at the church on Spring Street. They had a live nativity set up, and there were some alpacas and a donkey already there. Jacob was sleeping in the manger. Your tip about him liking alpacas paid off."

Mrs. Malloy laughed through her tears. "That's what I call a Christmas miracle. Thank you again."

Carson left them in the hands of the hospital staff and conferred with one of his deputies while Noelle waved goodbye to Jacob and waited in Carson's truck.

The adrenaline rush wore off, and Noelle was suddenly cold and very tired. When Carson opened the driver's door, she started to nod off. "Whew," he said, sliding behind the wheel. "I'm glad we got a happy ending tonight."

"Me too. I was so worried, especially since it was getting so late. Poor little guy."

"I'll run you back to the fire station to get the car, and then I need to go by the office to finish up the paperwork on all of this."

"Sounds good. I'm ready to call it a night. I'm exhausted."

"We'll sleep good tonight." He shuddered. "I'm just happy we found him, and he's okay. Missing kids is my worst nightmare, especially with all the coastline here. It's scary."

They arrived at the fire station and found it dark and locked. He walked her to the car, hugged her, and said, "I'll follow you back to town."

There was something comforting about seeing his headlights in the mirror and knowing he was watching out for her. By the time she drove down Front Street, it was quiet, and there were plenty of parking spaces, so she pulled right in front of the shop and noticed Carson waiting for her to get inside, his headlights making it easy to insert her key in the lock.

Once inside, she relocked the main door and waved at Carson, who blinked his lights at her.

She trudged upstairs, opted to skip what would be a very late dinner, and fell into bed.

———

Saturday morning, Noelle woke with her stomach growling. On the bedside table, her phone blinked, and she picked it up to find a text from Courtney. Her daughter wished her a happy birthday and included a cute photo of a dog wearing a birthday hat.

With all the drama last night, Noelle had forgotten all about her birthday. She opted to call her daughter instead of sending a reply. The call went to voicemail, so Noelle left her a thank you message and asked her to text when it might be a good time to chat.

Feeling a bit sad, she took a shower and decided to treat herself to a birthday breakfast. After a quick visit with Sam, who fixed her a birthday chai tea latte, she set out for the Front Street Café.

As she made her way to a table, she overheard the chatter around her, all of it focused on Jacob and his disappearance last night. The common sentiment was relief that he was safe.

As she ate her omelet and savored every bite of the home fries and homemade focaccia toast, she gazed out at the water. Last year at this time, she never imagined she'd be on an island looking for her birth mother.

Even if she didn't find the answers, Noelle was glad she'd come to Friday Harbor. The job Izzy mentioned was in the back of her mind. She could imagine herself living on the island. Having a circle of friends would be a welcome change from her rather anonymous life she led in Walla Walla.

It wasn't a bad life. It was just quiet and solitary. With the realization that Courtney wouldn't be coming home like she imagined, it held very little appeal. After Tom died, Noelle talked to him all the time. It comforted her and helped her when she was making choices, like the one to take the full-time professor job. It offered stability and retirement, which were two things she needed with a small daughter to raise on her own.

She liked Walla Walla and felt comfortable in her neighborhood and enjoyed the small downtown atmosphere. The only drawbacks were her lack of friends and hobbies. Chances are she could find some social clubs to join and activities to participate in and widen her circle, but here, it was effortless. She definitely needed a change and without anyone to keep her in Walla Walla, it sounded like a viable plan.

She hadn't talked to Tom in a very long time. He used to come to her in her dreams, especially those first few years. She couldn't remember the last time she dreamed of him. Noelle liked to believe after so long without him, her confidence had grown, and she didn't need him like she did in those early years. It reminded her of having an imaginary friend when she was little. It made her feel not so alone.

The more she thought about Tom, she pictured him smiling and telling her to follow her heart. To take a chance. She'd been responsible and pushed her needs aside to make Courtney her top priority. Her job gave her the security she craved, but in reality, it had become beyond monotonous. She taught the same classes year after year. The routine, which at first had been comforting, was now something she dreaded.

In the past, she considered a career change, but it was easier to stay where she was, add to her retirement benefits, and remain in the system. Now, with the ability to collect her retirement, it gave her the freedom to consider a change. She never imagined moving from Walla Walla, and she was too young to sit around and do nothing, but the job Izzy mentioned held the promise of something new.

As she thought about it and before she could talk herself out of it, she texted Izzy and asked her to keep her in the loop with regard to the position. Izzy and Blake had left for Yakima already, but she wanted to commit before she changed her mind. Moments later, Izzy replied with a text filled with happy emojis and a promise that she would check on the status when she returned next week. With a sense of triumph, Noelle lingered over another cup of tea before heading back to her apartment.

She had a few hours before she was due at the fire station for the wrapping party. She opted to tackle her laundry while she had spare time. The apartment had a stacked washer and dryer, both on the small side, so she settled in with a cup of tea and the mystery she was streaming after she put in the first load.

While she folded clothes, panic filled her. With only

Courtney to worry about for Christmas presents, she hadn't given a thought to buying things this year. She'd sent her gifts back with her at Thanksgiving. Now, with the invitations she had for Christmas Eve and Christmas, she needed to get a few things.

Her go-to gift was usually wine, but since Betty and Carson didn't drink, she'd have to think of something else. Wine would work for Amelia and Georgia. She could combine it with a charcuterie board, and it would be perfect for their evening.

She checked the time and had an hour before she was due at the fire station. She put her laundry away and grabbed her purse. Once downstairs, she headed down the sidewalk to do some window shopping.

First, she stopped by Lou's and ordered a charcuterie board for Christmas Eve. Carson mentioned they didn't need any food for their celebration, so she wandered to Kate's store, looking for inspiration.

The store was busy, and Kate was on the floor helping customers, and another woman was manning the register. Noelle wandered, hoping something would catch her eye.

She came upon a display of gorgeous photos, and, after checking the business card in the corner of the frame, Noelle realized they were Dean's. She was drawn to the breathtaking views of the coastline, the lighthouse, and the beautiful Christmas tree with the harbor in the background.

Carson's bare walls could use a little something and with Betty's love for the island, Noelle was sure she would appreciate one of them. She finally settled on her selections, adding one for herself and took them to the register.

Kate was working on it now, and her eyes widened when she looked up and saw Noelle. "How did you sneak in?"

"You're crazy busy today."

She nodded. "Lots of last-minute shoppers. I just stopped by for a few minutes to see how things were going, and I've been here for over two hours."

Noelle raised her hand. "Guilty of being one of those last-minute folks. I just remembered I needed a few things."

Kate offered to gift wrap them and wrapped each piece in tissue before placing them in festive holiday bags and adding gold ribbons. Noelle pointed at her photo of the Christmas tree. "That one is mine, so no wrapping needed."

Kate nodded and carried all of them to the counter. Noelle paid and collected her gifts. "Thank you, Kate. I'll see you later."

With a smile, Kate checked her watch. "We're bringing my son Mitch to help wrap. We'll see you as soon as I can break away."

"Wonderful. I look forward to meeting Mitch. See you there."

Noelle ran the gifts upstairs to her apartment and then hurried to the car. She didn't have time to get the wine and made a mental note to pick it up tomorrow.

With it being the weekend, the fire station was quieter today. Jeff was already there when she arrived and had situated the barrels by the wrapping tables. The coffee was brewed, and cocoa and tea were set up at the refreshment table. Even the cookie trays had been delivered.

She raised her brows at Jeff. "Someone has been a busy elf this morning. I'm sorry I wasn't here earlier."

"Aww, no problem. Sam helped me, and she just left to cover the shop. One of the girls isn't feeling well." He pointed at the barrels. "I left the food and personal items at the store, like we discussed. I'll deliver them to the senior center on Monday morning."

Before long, all the volunteers arrived, and the room was

abuzz with laughter and conversation as friends worked together to wrap dozens of pairs of socks and slippers, along with books and puzzles.

As Noelle sat at the end of the table, across from Spence and Kate, and next to Mitch, who was charming and kind like his mother, her heart warmed. She imagined a life on the island, surrounded by wonderful friends and a loving community.

While she was daydreaming, a hand on her shoulder startled her, and she looked up into the gentle brown eyes she'd come to look forward to seeing. Carson gripped her shoulder. "Where do you want me?"

She pointed at the space next to her. "Right here works."

He grabbed an empty chair and tied ribbons on the packages.

Noelle glanced over at him as he concentrated on a loop of ribbon. One more reason she'd fallen in love with the island sat next to her.

CHAPTER SIXTEEN

A few minutes before seven, a knock on her apartment door made Noelle quit fussing with her hair and hurry to answer it.

Carson greeted her with a wide smile and a bundle of white roses edged with pink. "Oh, my goodness, those are gorgeous. Thank you."

She rummaged in the cupboard and found a vase to put them in. She smiled and set them on the counter to admire them. "It's been a very long time since a man gave me flowers."

He stepped closer to her and put his arm around her. "A beautiful birthday girl deserves them. Especially one that's been volunteering and working on her big day."

She relished the warmth of his arm around her shoulders. "Today was actually fun. I had a good time."

He chuckled. "We better get going. I don't want to chance missing our reservation."

She reached for the new jacket she bought, and he held it for her as she slipped into it.

They walked down the street to The Bluff, where twinkling lights glimmered in the bushes surrounding the stairs leading to the restaurant. The hostess led them to a table with a superb view of the water and the town Christmas tree next to the harbor.

After they received the basket of warm bread with dipping oils and glasses of iced water, the two of them studied the menu. Their server took their drink orders and gave them a few minutes to make their selections.

As they waited for her to return, Carson pointed out the outdoor decks and eating areas. "We'll have to come back here this summer. They've got some of the best views in town."

She noted that he expected her to come back. Noelle gazed out the window, taking in the lights of the boats in the harbor, many still sporting their Christmas lights, and the moon reflecting off the dark water. "It's breathtaking."

He smiled from across the table. "Speaking of breathtaking, I forgot to tell you how gorgeous you look tonight. I'm a bit rusty at this, uh, dating thing."

"I'm beyond rusty." She took a sip from her wine glass. "You also look very handsome in your jacket. That blue is lovely on you."

He glanced down at the jacket he wore over his button-down white shirt. "I don't have occasion to dress up much."

"Me either." She touched the cowl of her dress. "I actually went shopping here and found this. I had nothing much to wear for a nice dinner."

"The color is really nice on you. It's perfect."

The server interrupted them and took their orders. Both of them opted for steak with potatoes and veggies. She thanked them and promised their clam chowders would be out soon.

The soup arrived, and Noelle savored the first creamy spoonful. "So good." After another taste, she met Carson's eyes. "Have you talked to Jacob's mom since Friday night?"

He nodded and took a sip from his Arnold Palmer. "I called her this morning. She and Jacob are both well."

"That's good. Such a scary situation."

"I think Mrs. Malloy is struggling a little with her husband deployed and the holidays. I invited them to stop by the sheriff's department on Christmas Eve. We always have a potluck for everyone who works there, along with their families. There are treats for the kids, and we show a movie for them in the squad room. I just don't want them to be alone, and a few of the deputies have kids his age."

"Aww, that's a wonderful tradition and idea. Did she sound like she would come?"

He nodded. "She actually did. I think Jacob's disappearance shook her up. Not that having a husband in law enforcement is quite the same, but I think she'll find some camaraderie with some of the deputies' wives, especially ones with young children. She just needs a friend group right now."

Noelle reached across the table and held his hand. "You really are a good man, Carson."

He blushed as a slow smile lifted the corner of his lips. "I like helping people, especially those like Jacob and his mom. They deserve a little grace."

Their entrees arrived and after admiring the platters of food in front of them, they dug into the juicy steaks and buttery potatoes. As Noelle cut another piece off her steak, she looked across the table. "This is beyond yummy. How's yours?"

"Perfect," said Carson, spearing another bite with his fork. "I haven't eaten here yet. It's not exactly a place that caters to solo diners. I'm so glad I had a reason to come tonight, with you."

"I don't remember the last time I had such an elegant birthday treat. Thank you for all of this."

When they finished their meal, a busser collected their plates and a few minutes later, their server arrived and placed a long plate in the middle of the table. A tall sparkler shimmered atop a huge slice of chocolate cake.

She placed two forks on the platter and winked at Noelle. "Happy Birthday. Enjoy."

The sparkler sputtered and eventually extinguished itself. Noelle glanced up at Carson, who sported a grin, clearly pleased with himself and the birthday surprise. He pointed at the cake. "It's six layers of chocolate with fudge frosting and walnuts."

Her mouth gaped. "I'm stuffed. It looks so good, but I'll never be able to eat much of it."

He picked up his fork. "Just take a bite or two, and we'll take the rest with us."

She eased her fork into the thick frosting and let the first bite melt in her mouth. It was rich and decadent. Everything a birthday should be.

After two bites, she put down her fork. "It's so good, but I can't manage any more. We'll have to save it for later."

Carson slipped one more bite onto his fork and nodded. "I'll ask her to box it up for us."

After he paid the check, he carried the takeout box and offered Noelle his arm as they strolled along the harbor. "Boy oh boy," she said. "I could get used to this view."

"It definitely is one of the perks of living here."

"Have you ever thought about leaving?"

He shrugged. "Not really. This is my home. I've always

enjoyed the small-town life and being close to Mom and Dad. It's comforting. It's where I belong."

"I can see that. You're a beloved figure in the community. People respect you and look up to you. They count on you."

"I guess all of that is true, but it's more about the connection I feel to this place. It's what I know. What I love. I can't imagine ever leaving."

"Home. It's that feeling when you know you're exactly where you should be with the people you love most."

He smiled and when she looked down, she noticed they were holding hands. She took delight in the feel of her hand in his. They wandered the length of the street, admiring the lights and stopping by the Christmas tree on their way back to her apartment.

Noelle unlocked the door. "You've got to come in and help me eat the rest of that cake. I'll make some coffee or tea."

"Either works," he said, following her inside and helping her with her jacket.

She went about filling the kettle and gathering two mugs and plates for their cake. "I've been watching a really good mystery series. You might like it." She told him more about the series set in New Zealand that featured a charming police detective who loved country music.

"Sounds good to me," he said, carrying their cake plates as he took a seat on the couch.

She brought the mugs of tea and joined him. They watched an episode and enjoyed the antics of the odd characters who lived in the small town where the murder was committed.

That led her to ask about violent crime on the island.

"The last murder we had was in 2016. A husband killed his wife. We don't have many here. We did have a young man die from fentanyl poisoning last year. We found the person who gave it to him, but he would never divulge where he obtained it. It's a real problem nationwide and has reached our peaceful shores. I hate it."

They'd managed to eat the cake and drink a pot of tea while they watched and visited. She took their plates into the kitchen and refilled the kettle.

"Where's Justice tonight?" she asked, handing him a fresh mug.

"She's having a sleepover at Mom's." He grinned and put his mug on the side table.

After a few moments of silence, he cleared his throat. "You mentioned you were rusty at dating and lost your husband long ago. Have you or should I say would you consider a serious relationship?" The man who solved problems and made split second decisions, stammered. "I, uh, I mean, with me."

His bumbling delivery made her grin, but she hid it as she took a sip from her mug. He was endearing and oh so genuine. "I've never met someone like you. I absolutely would consider it. You do realize we live three hundred and fifty miles apart, right? And, fair warning, I've been alone for a long time, and I'm pretty sure dating and relationships are not my strong suit."

He tilted his head back and laughed. "I understand the distance is tough. Yeah, I'm right there with you. I've poured all my energy into my work. Years ago, well over a decade now, I had a serious relationship with a woman who lived here at the time. She was a freelance journalist and took a job offer for a big paper in Chicago. She didn't even tell me she applied or was looking to leave. She assumed I'd be gung-ho to follow her."

He sighed and reached for his tea. "Needless to say, it

soured me on the whole serious relationship idea, and I abandoned it and focused on work. It was more predictable."

"Well, I never even tried. After Tom died, I was lost and scared. I tried to put on a good front for Courtney but cried myself to sleep for months. I was working part-time at the college, stressed about finances and everything else, and when a full-time position opened, I jumped on it. My goal was to keep our life the same, as much as possible. I didn't want Courtney to suffer or go without and was determined to keep our house."

"You mentioned retirement. Are you serious about that?"

She shrugged. "I think I am. Now more than ever." She told him about the job Izzy mentioned.

His eyes widened. "Izzy always has the scoop. Are you considering applying for it?"

She grinned. "I am. I'm not ready to retire-retire, but a change would be wonderful. I'm burnt out, bored, and there's nothing for me in Walla Walla now."

"That makes the idea of exploring a relationship much easier." He grinned and raised his brows.

"It's a bit of a longshot, I'm sure, but I'm ready for a new chapter."

He tilted his head. "I think with your experience and qualifications, it really isn't a longshot. People love to come and visit the island, but there aren't many who want to move here."

She gazed out the window and then met his eyes. "I'd love nothing more."

He bent his head closer and brushed his lips over hers. She closed her eyes and breathed in the woodsy scent along his neck. She could get used to the feeling of his arms around her.

CHAPTER SEVENTEEN

Noelle had a lazy and relaxing Sunday. She spent much of her day combing through online sites to locate the major hospitals in Washington that were active fifty years ago. She hoped to have information from Bunny after Christmas, but if her Bellingham contact came up empty, Noelle wanted to be ready to contact other regional hospitals.

She tried to find birth records online but didn't have much luck. She made a note to ask Bunny about searching other newspapers in Washington for birth records. She assumed she had colleagues in Seattle and other cities that might be able to help. She also added the archives in Olympia and the historical society in Tacoma as places to look.

Late in the afternoon, her phone rang. After talking to Courtney for a few minutes and hearing all about the fun she was having on her break and how wonderful Phil's family was, she trudged downstairs and collected a brownie and a latte and made that her dinner.

Tomorrow morning was the party at the senior center. She scrolled her calendar and smiled. Normally, it was blank, but it was filled with fun activities over the next week. It would be difficult to go home to her mundane life after the new year.

As she crawled into bed, she couldn't resist opening her laptop one more time. She clicked on the file with her resume, which she kept up to date like she taught her students, and tweaked a few things, freshening it and getting it ready to submit with whatever application she might need.

After Carson's revelation last night, she was even more excited about the prospect of a new job and a new life.

Monday, Noelle was up early and opted to take a walk before getting ready for the party. The sun was shining in the blue sky, and it was shaping up to be a gorgeous day. As she walked along the harbor, she imagined being able to do this every morning and the more she thought about it, Noelle pictured herself living close to downtown.

As she walked by the market, she remembered the wine she intended to take on Christmas Eve and detoured in to get several bottles. She lugged them home in the cardboard carrier they gave her and jumped in the shower.

Dressed in jeans and a dark-green sweater, she set out for the senior center. When she walked in, she noticed Amelia and Georgia busy adding festive centerpieces to the dining tables. She waved at them and wandered over to where Jeff and one of his staff members were wrestling one of the barrels of gifts into position.

Jeff smiled at Noelle and sent his helper back to the store.

"That's the last one. Carmen told us where to station these, so I think you're set."

"Thanks again, Jeff. I appreciate all the work you put into helping with this and the kids' party."

"Happy to do it."

When Carson joined them, Carmen came up to greet them and handed Carson a bright-green apron. "We're so glad to see you, Sheriff Mercer. I can't thank you enough for donating the prime rib for today's luncheon. It's a favorite around here, as are you."

"My pleasure, really. Today is one of my favorite days of the year."

She thanked him again before rushing off to tend to someone calling for her. As she and Carson chatted with Amelia and Georgia, a man using a walker and a woman came from the entrance and joined them.

Amelia greeted them both with a hug. "Noelle, please meet Henry and Doris. They are my good friends who live just down the street. Doris plays the piano and will be entertaining us soon."

Henry extended his hand. "Pleasure to meet you, Noelle. You have a very fitting name for the season."

"Lovely to meet both of you," she said, shaking, Doris' hand next.

Amelia pointed at the table nearest the piano. "If you're staying for lunch, you should sit with us, Noelle."

"I'd love to, thanks. I'll leave my bag there while I tend to the gifts."

Carson nodded. "I've got waiter duties today but will join you when I'm done."

More and more people arrived, all of them decked out in Christmas sweaters or festive ties and scarves. While they waited for the party to begin, Amelia and Georgia served coffee and tea to anyone who wanted it.

In the midst of that, Carmen took to the microphone and explained they would be passing out Christmas gifts to everyone, and they had a table set up near the entrance with lots of personal care and food items that were free for the taking.

The crowd burst into applause, and Noelle began her task of delivering wrapped packages to each of the tables. Carson pitched in to help while Amelia and Georgia and a few others kept the beverages flowing.

Doris played upbeat holiday songs that got the whole room clapping and singing along to the festive music. Noelle held back tears as she handed presents to the grateful men and women, who asked for very little and were overjoyed with the simplest of gifts.

After some slipper trading of sizes and a few other exchanges between some of the attendees, everyone had something they loved. After another round of carols, servers circled through the room with cups of soup.

Along with Sheriff Mercer, Carmen made a point of introducing the mayor and a few council members who arrived to help serve lunch and thanked them all for their support. Noelle was more than a little interested in checking out the mayor, who was in his first term and seemed like a sincere man, visiting with everyone as he handed out plates.

Noelle slipped into the chair next to Henry and ate the surprisingly good potato leek soup. It was followed by the main entrée, which was received with eager gasps from each table. Prime rib, mashed potatoes, gravy, veggies, applesauce, and a fluffy roll with butter were delivered by none other than their favorite sheriff.

He wheeled his cart of meal trays away and promised to be back when he was done serving to join them.

Within a few minutes, Carson, still wearing his apron, settled into the chair next to Noelle with his plate of food. She pointed at her half-eaten meal. "It's really good. I'm impressed."

He winked. "They do a great job here, and this is one of their special meals. Not the norm."

As he ate, several of the attendees stopped by to pat him on the back and thank him for donating the prime rib. He even got several hugs from the women in the group.

Noelle chuckled and bent close to his ear and whispered, "Are you running for re-election by any chance?"

He grinned and shook his head. "Not this year. I just got re-elected in November to my third term, and I've been unopposed each time I've run."

"Wow," she said, her eyes wide. "I'm impressed."

As they ate, Noelle learned that Henry had lived on the island since the 1960s, and Doris had also lived on the island for most of her life. As Carson finished his meal, a volunteer wheeled a tray of desserts to the table.

Henry's smile grew wider when she handed him a piece of pumpkin pie with whipped cream. Doris excused herself to play more carols and made Henry promise not to eat her pie while she was gone.

As some of the seniors gathered their belongings, Noelle left the table to help them collect any of the food or personal care items they wanted to take home. The market donated some reusable bags, and Noelle, Amelia, and Georgia helped gather things for them, while Carson and a few other volunteers carried them out to their cars.

By the time the party ended, they still had a huge

collection of items, and Amelia eyed the table filled with paper goods and other products. She glanced over at Georgia. "We may have to make more than one trip to get all of this delivered, along with our normal food boxes."

"Good thing we're starting early." Georgia smiled and stacked the boxes of toothpaste together.

Amelia sighed. "Just getting it all loaded in my SUV to take to the food bank will take more than one trip."

Noelle pointed at the empty barrels that held the wrapped gifts. "Jeff is coming back to get the barrels, I'm sure he wouldn't mind loading what you can't fit in your SUV and dropping it on the way."

She checked her watch. "He's due here in a few minutes."

Amelia nodded. "Good idea. That will save us some time and get us out of here so they can close."

No sooner than she uttered his name, Jeff walked through the door. He and Carson managed to load everything into Amelia's SUV and Jeff's truck before Carson had to leave and get back to the office.

Noelle walked with him to his truck. "Thanks for all your help. It was such a nice day."

He smiled. "Like I said, always one of my favorites. I'm working most of tomorrow, but how about we meet for a Christmas Eve coffee at Sam's in the morning before I head to work?"

"Sounds perfect. I'll see you then."

She made her way back to the building, collected her handbag, and checked in with Carmen before driving back to her apartment.

She kicked off her shoes and fell onto the couch. It had been a long and busy day, but it left her filled with gratitude and the spirit of the season.

With a sense of accomplishment that her volunteer work was done, not to mention a happy heart at having played a small part in making Christmas a bit brighter for so many deserving residents, she turned on the television for some background noise and let herself surrender to the temptation of a late-afternoon nap.

CHAPTER EIGHTEEN

Despite the nap and a good night's rest, Noelle overslept on Christmas Eve morning. She blinked at the clock and in a panic, remembered her coffee date with Carson. She had no time for a shower or much of anything else.

After she threw on her exercise pants and a sweatshirt and brushed her teeth, she opted for a winter hat that would hide her messy hair and rushed downstairs.

As she came from the stairs, Carson came through the door. She breathed a sigh of relief that he wasn't sitting there waiting for her.

Being a true gentleman, he didn't comment on her disheveled appearance. He insisted on treating her and added one of the warm cinnamon rolls that had just been delivered from the bakery to their drink order.

While they waited for their order, Noelle glanced out the window. "Where's Justice?"

"I dropped her at my office on my way here. She's got a comfy spot there and has everyone wrapped around her finger. With the department holiday potluck, she'll be in heaven. Lots of the deputies have kids, and she loves all the littles."

"That sounds like a full day."

"It's always fun, and then I'm working tonight. I like to take the swing shift and let those with families have time with them. Usually, it's one of our quieter nights on the island."

With wide eyes, Noelle smiled at him. "That's admirable. I'm sure they appreciate it."

"I like to give the guys a break when I can, and I'll be off all day tomorrow."

He carried the huge cinnamon roll and two forks to their table. He raised his cup to her. "Thanks again for pitching in and taking the lead on the donation projects. You really saved my bacon."

She laughed. "It was fun. Despite losing a little boy and Santa breaking his arm, I had a good time. Especially yesterday. It was a great day."

"We have some wonderful people who have lived here for decades. They're the backbone of this island—some of my absolute favorites."

"I thought your mom might be there."

He chuckled. "She thinks the senior center is for old people."

That made Noelle smile. "She's a lovely person. We had a nice chat when I drove her home the other night."

"She's got a soft spot for you, Noelle. I think she bonded with you as a baby and never really got over having to give you to the social services people. Seeing you and having you here has ignited a new spark in her."

Noelle brought her hand to her chest. "Aww, that's so sweet. She's a wonderful mother. Betty was so kind and told me she was sure my birth mom was doing what she thought best at the time."

He reached for her hand and held it. "I'm sure she was."

With a shrug, Noelle nodded. "I had wonderful parents and a childhood most would envy. I never imagined being here, looking for my roots. Sometimes, I wonder why my mom even left me that information. She didn't have to."

"I would imagine it's something she wanted to do for a long time but was scared. I'm sure the longer it went on without them telling you, the harder it became. She probably wanted you to have a family if you wanted to seek them out. In passing, she wanted to let go of the secret and let you have the whole story and give you the option."

She pondered his words for a few seconds. "I guess I can see that. It's just hard to wrap my head around all of this."

He raised his brows at her. "I, for one, am so glad your mom left you that note. Otherwise, we would have never met. You wouldn't be here. I would have been stuck with all the work on the donation drives myself, and you wouldn't be contemplating a new career and move."

With a laugh, she grinned at him. "You're right, of course." She took a sip from her latte. "Last night, I finally accepted that I may not ever find my birth mother, and I think I'm okay with that. Like you said, my quest brought me here, and I've found new friends who feel like family and a place I love. For the first time in a long time, I'm excited about the future."

"Then, I say your mom gave you the best gift she could."

After another bite from the cinnamon roll, he glanced over at her. "You're going to Noah's tonight, right?"

"Yes, I'm looking forward to that. I told myself I need to curb my enthusiasm about his books, though. I have to dial down my fascination."

"I'm sure you'll have a wonderful time. Georgia and Dale are great, as is Amelia. I think you'll love Noah's place, too."

She gasped and said, "I need to pick up the charcuterie board I ordered. I'm glad you mentioned the party. Lou's is only open a couple of hours today."

"Well, I need to get a move on and get to work, anyway. I hope you have a great day and can't wait to see you tomorrow. Come out anytime; we'll be in the kitchen early."

"Thanks, Carson. I've been looking forward to it all week."

As he left, she darted upstairs and got ready for the day. Once dressed, she hurried to Lou's and picked up the gorgeous charcuterie board. She wished Andi, who was manning the register, a Merry Christmas and tucked the appetizer into the fridge.

It was odd to have nothing to do on Christmas Eve. She was used to cooking and baking with Courtney and her mom. It was always a joyful time, and she missed the busyness of it all.

Instead, and in honor of Noah, she opened her tablet and pulled up his new release that she hadn't had time to finish and settled in with a cup of tea.

After she read the last page of Noah's excellent book, Noelle refilled her mug and sat, admiring her Christmas tree. She was fifty-years old, and it didn't sound too bad until she realized less than half of her life was before her.

This time of year was one of nostalgia, and this year, without her mom, it was a stark reminder of the limited time Noelle had left. She'd spent most of her adult life focused on earning money, providing a stable home for her daughter, saving for college, and spending any extra time with her parents. With the hope of Courtney returning to Walla Walla gone, she had no reason to continue, stuck in the same rut.

Now, before her was the chance to do something for herself. Something that wasn't totally planned. It was more than a little scary, but that note her mother left her taught her that change could actually be wonderful.

The idea of retirement sounded good, but she would never have given it serious consideration before coming to the island. She would have plugged along at her job, stayed in Walla Walla without the dream or hope of a different future. Most of the change she'd experienced in her life hadn't been welcome and had been hard.

The possibilities this trip brought, all because her mother shared the story of her birth, weren't only exciting, but they held the potential for Noelle to reinvent her life. She could have more than the drudgery her job had become and an empty house. She might even have a full and thriving life.

An actual relationship with someone like Carson was beyond her wildest imagination. Even if it didn't lead to anything serious, she knew they would be friends, and together, with the others who had welcomed her, it made the idea of leaving all she'd known easy.

She hoped Izzy and Carson were right and that her experience and qualifications were the right fit for the mayor. If not, she could still retire and move, but having a job would make it much easier.

Thinking about the past prompted her to call Courtney. When her daughter answered, Noelle's spirits lifted. With all the background noise, they didn't talk long, but it was comforting to hear her daughter's voice. She even sent a text with a photo of the enormous tree at Phil's family's vacation home. The happiness in Courtney's voice and her enthusiasm filled Noelle's heart with joy for her daughter.

As much as she missed her, there was nothing better than knowing her beloved daughter was happy. She only hoped she knew what she was doing when it came to accepting Phil's proposal. Noelle barely knew the guy, so she couldn't judge him, but it seemed too fast.

Too soon.

Noelle learned long ago not to push Courtney, but she hoped their engagement would be a long one and give them more time to get to know each other better and be sure of their desire to spend the rest of their lives together. She also remembered marrying Tom when she was very young. Her parents gently questioned her but didn't stand in her way.

Back then, she didn't think she was too young. Now, with the shoe on the other foot, it wasn't as easy. She treasured her parents even more for letting her make her own decisions. She would have to do the same for Courtney, but it was harder than she thought.

After she disconnected, Noelle changed into a warm sweater with a pretty snowflake embroidered into it. Amelia assured her the gathering was casual, and everyone was wearing jeans. She touched up her hair and toted the wine down to the car and then carried the charcuterie board and placed it in the backseat.

It wasn't yet dark, which made for an easier trip. She followed the directions Carson gave her, which included landmarks, and took the turn for Noah's neighborhood. When the house came into view, she gasped. The roofline twinkled with lights and gave it an inviting, holiday feel.

Before she could unload her things, Amelia appeared at her side. "Let me help you." Noelle handed her the charcuterie board and took the wine.

"Oh," said Amelia, eyeing the board. "This looks so good. You really didn't have to bring anything, but I'm excited to dig into this."

They climbed the steps to the stone porch that ran the length of the house. "This is a gorgeous home."

"With a lead from Jeff, Noah found it. He really loves it and says he gets more writing done here than he ever has." She pointed at the sky. "You're just in time to see the best part of the place. The sunsets."

Georgia welcomed her with a warm hug, and Dale did the same. Noah extended his hand and introduced his son Will. Noelle thanked them all for having her and after placing her contributions in the kitchen, Amelia led her to the back patio, where Georgia introduced her to her sister of the heart Harry and her husband Clay. They were visiting from Lavender Valley.

A dramatic orange and gold glow hovered below a band of deep-blue clouds. Noelle sucked in her breath. "That's stunning. I can see what you mean about this being your favorite part of the house."

Noah put his arm around Amelia. "We love sitting out here in the evenings. I wish we had a total water view, but this little slice is hard to beat."

They stood, watching until the last bit of gold disappeared into the dark water. "I would never tire of watching that," said Noelle.

Amelia led them back inside, and she and Georgia set out platters of appetizers on the kitchen island counter. "This is a serve yourself kind of affair," said Amelia, pointing at the stack of plates and wrapped silverware.

As Noelle waited for her turn, she couldn't resist turning to Noah behind her. "I just finished your new book, and I have to say, it's one of your best."

"Thank you. I'm so glad you liked it. That reminds me, I have some signed copies for you to take with you, so don't let me forget."

"Wow, my Christmas is made. That's very kind of you."

She filled her plate and joined the others who were gathered in the dining room. Amelia poured herself a glass of wine and offered some to Noelle. She held up her hand. "Just a splash. I'm driving home and don't want to risk a problem."

Amelia obliged, pouring a couple of sips into her glass and refilling Georgia's. Clay and Harry entertained them with stories about the ranch and the lavender farm and told them how much they loved the island.

After another nibble from the charcuterie board, Amelia pointed at the window seat and a stack of boxes. "We've got some movies, if anyone is interested, and tons of board games and puzzles to play. Whatever anybody is up for."

After more snacks, they settled on a puzzle, which was relaxing and let everyone play and take breaks as they liked. When they finished it, Amelia brought out the cards, and they played a competitive game of Rummy.

After dessert, Georgia and Dale gathered their things and, together with Clay and Harry, said their goodbyes. Noelle opted to follow them on the roads she wasn't familiar with, especially in the dark. She thanked Noah for his hospitality and hugged Amelia before steering her car behind Dale's, where he was waiting at the end of the driveway for her.

She followed them until they took the turn for the golf community. He flashed his lights at her, and she did the same. From there, it was an easy drive downtown. She parked in front of the coffee shop and couldn't resist a stop at the town tree by the harbor.

The view of its colorful lights with the water in the background and the tranquil sky littered with stars above was pure perfection. Instead of spending Christmas Eve alone, she'd enjoyed the conversation and company of wonderful friends.

Although she'd come on a quest for her past, she'd found so much more on the tiny island.

CHAPTER NINETEEN

Christmas Day, Noelle indulged in a leftover piece of hot chocolate cake with marshmallow filling for breakfast. Georgia insisted she take a slab of it home last night and although far from healthy, it was sinfully delicious.

It had been a lovely evening and after the ladies won the right to pick the movie, which was one of her guilty pleasures, *The Holiday*, Noelle was home and tucked in bed well before midnight.

Noelle finished her pot of tea and selected the cranberry sweater she wore each Christmas. Her mom gave it to her years ago and the soft chenille fabric was a favorite of hers. It made her feel like her mom was with her for the holiday.

She wasn't quite ready to go to Carson's yet, but Noelle collected the gift bags from Kate's store—the third one contained a few dog toys and treats for Justice—to put in the car so she wouldn't forget them. When she opened her apartment door, she found a Christmas stocking propped in the corner. She smiled at the sweet gesture.

After putting the gifts in the car, she hurried upstairs, anxious to find out what was in the stocking.

She carried the heavy velvet stocking to the couch and reached inside. There was a gift card to Sam's shop, along with a pretty cup painted with a scene of the harbor. A bag of cinnamon candy canes and tin of tea rounded out her treats. The tin had a small tag on it where Sam and Jeff signed their names and wished her a Merry Christmas.

Noelle's heart warmed at their thoughtful gift. In all her years at home, nobody outside of her family ever surprised her with treats on Christmas morning. She texted Sam a quick thank you and wished her and Jeff a Merry Christmas.

After tidying the kitchen, she collected her handbag and set out for Carson's house. When she pulled to the gate, she pushed the button, and, within seconds, it opened for her.

She pulled behind Betty's car and before she could open her door, Carson was standing at it. He opened it for her and said, "Merry Christmas."

Noelle smiled at him and took the hand he offered her. "Merry Christmas to you." She opened the backdoor and collected the gift bags.

He raised his brows as he eyed them. "What do you have there?"

"Santa stopped by and left these for you and your mom." She pointed at the smaller one. "This one is for Justice, so you might want to put it where she can't grab it."

He took it, shook his head, and smiled. "You're naughty. I'm pretty certain we said don't bring anything."

She shrugged. "I can't say no to Santa."

He put his arm around her as they walked to the door. "I'm so happy you're here."

She looked up at him. "Me, too. There's no place I'd rather be."

Justice greeted her with quick wags of her tail and a wiggling bum. Carson urged the dog out of the way, welcomed Noelle inside, and took her coat. She deposited the gift bags under the tree and turned to find Betty in the kitchen, wearing a Christmas apron. The petite woman greeted her with a firm and long hug. "Merry Christmas, dear."

A hint of rosemary and orange permeated the air. "Something smells delicious."

"We're doing a spiral ham and a turkey breast today. We couldn't decide, so we opted for both. That way, we'll have plenty of leftovers."

Carson let Justice have one of her new toys, a stuffed otter that squeaked, and made sure she knew it was from Noelle. The dog scampered off with it, tail wagging. He offered Noelle something to drink, and she opted for orange juice and a cup of tea. He pointed at the cake plate on the island counter. "Mom made her famous eggnog cake."

"Oh, that looks so pretty," said Noelle, marveling at the professional-looking white frosting.

He clapped his hands together. "I'm starving. Is everybody ready for brunch?"

Betty and Noelle both nodded and pitched in to help him get the egg casserole and pan of pecan-studded sweet rolls, bubbling in caramelized sugar and cinnamon, from the oven. Carson added a fruit salad from the fridge and urged his guests to fill their plates.

Noelle took her first bite of the egg casserole. "This is really yummy. I love the sausage in it."

He glanced at his mom. "All the recipes are Mom's but thank you. I just followed her directions."

"Well, everything is delicious," said Noelle, spearing another piece of the pecan roll.

"How was your night at Noah's?" asked Carson.

"It was fun, and you way undersold his place. It's magnificent. I got there in time for a sunset."

"Yeah, it's a nice property. He's got a nice view there."

"How was your potluck and your night at work?"

"The potluck was great. Jacob and his mom came, and I think Mrs. Malloy made a few new friends, as did Jacob. They seemed much happier." He took a swallow from his cup of coffee. "Work was relatively quiet. A couple of high school kids were stealing some decorations from yards, but that was about the extent of the crime wave."

She chuckled. "How about you, Betty? Did you do anything special?"

"I went to a friend's house for the afternoon. One of the ladies from church had a few of us over. We played cards and ate, of course. I need to go on a diet when the holidays are over."

Noelle rolled her eyes. "You and me both. I haven't been brave enough to step on a scale, but I can tell it's time to cut back."

Carson chuckled. "You've still got a few more parties before you leave."

"Yeah, I'm going to get strict about it once I get home. It will be easier there without the temptation of all these social gatherings and the aroma of fresh baked brownies in my house."

After they finished, Noelle volunteered to do the dishes while Carson packed away the leftovers. Once all the dishes were done and the counter tidied, Carson pointed at the living room. "We've got some time before I have to start working on the potatoes for dinner. We can watch something or take a walk, whatever sounds good."

Betty took a cup of tea into the living room, and Noelle

made her way to the Christmas tree, where Justice was napping, but opened an eye to investigate what she was doing. She gave the dog a pat on the head and collected the gifts she brought. "I know you said I didn't need to bring anything, but I couldn't come empty-handed." She handed each of them a gift bag.

With a quick smile, Betty opened hers. "I love gifts." She unwrapped the tissue and held the frame up so Carson could see the stunning photo of the sunset over the harbor. "That's gorgeous. I love it. Thank you, Noelle. That's so kind of you."

Carson opened his and smiled. "I love it. Thank you." He held up the photo of a lone kayaker along the rugged and tree-studded coastline. "I think this was taken near the resort Jeff's family owns. It's a great kayaking spot."

Noelle sighed. "You've both given me so much. I couldn't think of anything to get you that would be equal to the love you've shown me. I will be forever grateful."

Betty dabbed at her eyes with a napkin.

Carson plucked an envelope from one of the branches of the tree. "Mom and I wanted to get you something too. This is a little out there, but it's something you can think about and if it doesn't work, don't worry."

With a questioning look, she took the red envelope.

Inside the glittery card was a note that entitled her to the pick of the litter from golden retriever puppies that would be born in March and ready for their forever homes in late May. Carson added a note that he was willing to care for the puppy until Noelle moved to the island or deliver it to her in Walla Walla if she decided to stay there.

Included were pictures of the prior pups from the breeder and as Noelle gazed at them, her heart melted.

With watery eyes, she looked over at Betty and then up at

Carson. "That's so sweet. They're adorable. Irresistible, in fact."

Carson grinned at her. "I know how much you miss your dog, and Mom and I thought it would be wonderful for you to have a new best friend. But, like I said, if you decide against it, it's not a problem. This is the same breeder where I got Justice."

Tears stung her eyes, and Noelle stepped toward Carson and hugged him. "This is so thoughtful. I've been wanting a dog but wasn't sure. It's so hard to lose them."

He squeezed her tight and nodded. "I know, but they make life so much better."

She turned toward Betty. "This is just the nicest gift I've ever gotten. Thank you both so very much."

Betty smiled and pointed at her son. "This was all Carson's doing."

Noelle's heart warmed at the joy on his face, and she couldn't wait to meet her new furry friend.

Betty rose from her chair. "I think I'm going to grab a quick nap before we start on dinner prep."

"We'll probably take Justice for a walk but will be back in plenty of time to peel potatoes. You just rest and relax, Mom."

She waved as she made her way down the hallway to the guestroom.

Before they could get their jackets on, Justice was at the door, ready to go. Carson chuckled and opened the door.

They wandered around his property and then down the driveway and through the neighborhood, which was covered in thick trees, with most houses set far back from the street.

As they walked, Carson held her hand. "I've got one more surprise for you."

Her eyes widened. "I'm not sure you can top a puppy."

"I didn't want to overstep, but I took the liberty of mentioning you to the mayor after the party at the senior center. I let him know you were interested in the job that would be coming up and touted your experience and qualifications."

She sucked in a breath. "Wow."

"He and I get along well, and he was excited to know you're interested. He's worried about filling the position. He wants to meet you before you go back home."

"Really?" Her voice betrayed her excitement.

He nodded. "Yes. He's in and out this week but will be in the office tomorrow morning. He said just stop by. You don't need an appointment."

"Oh, my gosh. Okay, this might be really close to a puppy." She squeezed his hand tighter. "That is great news. Now, I just have to impress him."

He brought her hand to his lips and kissed the top of it. "That will be a piece of cake."

She would miss this guy when she went back to Walla Walla. Now, more than ever, she wanted this job to work out.

CHAPTER TWENTY

The next morning, she met Carson at his office where she printed out a copy of her resume on heavy paper she picked up at the office supply store. Dressed in the most professional-looking suit she had with her, she placed her resume in the plastic portfolio she bought and took a deep breath.

Carson assured her she looked terrific, and she set out for the mayor's office in the same complex as Carson's department. With shaking hands, she stepped into the reception room of the mayor's suite. The desk was empty, and the mayor's office door to the right of it stood open.

She walked across the wooden floor and knocked on the door, cringing at the thought of interrupting him, unannounced.

Moments later, a man in jeans and a polo shirt came to the doorway. "You must be the Ms. Davis Sheriff Mercer told me about. Please come in. I'm David Williams, and you can call me Dave."

She returned his handshake and took a seat in front of his

desk. "I appreciate your willingness to meet me today. I know it's a busy time of year."

He smiled and waved away her concern. "It's actually nice and quiet. My secretary is off until after the first of the year, and I'm not working much, but what Carson told me piqued my interest."

The mayor went on to explain the expertise he was hoping to find in a candidate and asked her a few questions. They spoke for about twenty minutes, and the more Noelle talked with him, the more she liked him. He was calm and came across as a genuine and down-to-earth person. He was also a long-time businessman and understood numbers. He was impressed that she'd done her homework and looked at their budget documents online. She offered him her resume, and he eagerly accepted it.

"As soon as we post the position, I'll be sure to let you know. We're used to doing interviews remotely over video, so the process shouldn't be too burdensome. I hope to make a final decision in April, so the person we hire has time to relocate and be here in mid-June. I'd like whoever it is to work with Rhonda before she retires."

"That makes good sense to me. I'm working until the beginning of June, but if I know in April, I'd have no problem being here in mid-June."

He smiled at her and rose from his chair. "That sounds terrific, Noelle. I'm so glad we were able to meet before you left."

He walked her to the door and promised to keep in touch. She let out a long breath, confident she'd made a good impression and that the job duties he described were all things she would have no problem doing. She made her way back to the sheriff's office. Carson's vehicle was gone, so she didn't bother going inside and drove back to the apartment.

Having skipped breakfast, she was starving and after changing into jeans and a sweater, Noelle walked over to the Front Street Café and indulged in a tasty breakfast. After she lingered over her cup of tea, she wandered back to the apartment and made a list of everything she would need to do, if by some miracle, she got the job and had to move by June.

When Carson picked her up a few minutes before four, when they were due at Jack and Lulu's house, Noelle couldn't wait to tell him all about her visit with the mayor.

He turned just after Lime Kiln State Park and when Carson pulled in front of the house, she was still chattering on about it. He turned off the ignition and grinned at her. "I'm so glad you're excited about the idea of moving."

"I liked him, and I think working there would be terrific. Just the change I'm looking for."

He took her hand as they made their way to the house. She lifted her head and gazed out to notice the stunning water view. "Wow, this is gorgeous."

Jack answered the door and welcomed them inside. The cheerful voices and laughter drew them toward the kitchen, but Noelle couldn't help but stand with her mouth agape in the entryway. It was like stepping into the pages of one of those architectural magazines. Tasteful artwork and photos decorated the walls, and the high ceilings made the space feel enormous. The gorgeous blue water was visible from the tall glass doors along the living area.

Jack led the way past the floor-to-ceiling fireplace that separated the living area from the kitchen. Everyone was gathered around the dining table and huge granite island.

Jack reached for the hand of a woman with stylish gray hair, dressed in slim black leggings and a vibrant blue silky tunic that matched her pretty eyes.

"This is my beautiful wife Lulu."

She hugged Carson and grasped Noelle's extended hand between both of hers. "Such a pleasure to meet you." Lulu held Noelle's gaze for several seconds. "Welcome, please come in and get something to drink. Our guest of honor isn't here yet."

Lulu urged Noelle further into the kitchen and poured her a glass of wine. Kate, Sam, and Izzy were busy helping to get the food organized. Noelle gazed out the door off the dining room and spotted Amelia on the huge, covered patio, which was more like an outdoor living room.

Noah and Will stood further down on the lawn, pointing out toward the water.

As Lulu passed by her, Noelle turned and said, "Your home is lovely. What a gorgeous yard and view."

"Jack snagged this one several years ago, and I told him, I'm not moving again. It's perfect for us." She pointed toward the living area. "Feel free to wander. Nate and Regi and little Emma are on their way."

Noelle couldn't resist the offer and took her wine as she wandered past the living room to the master suite, which was a huge space that she guessed was half the size of her entire house. There was plenty of room for an oversized ottoman and footstool with a bookcase behind it, a desk, and an exercise bike. The room was done in tasteful neutrals with splashes of blues that mimicked the different colors of the sea out the window.

Noelle loved the window seat where comfy pillows were stacked atop a cushion and built-in bookcases flanked both sides. It was the perfect reading cove.

A huge bathroom with a walk-in shower and soaking tub, plus his and her walk-in closets rounded out the space.

As Noelle left, the framed family photos on the wall caught her eye. A very young Lulu and Jack posed with a brood of children. One boy, which must be Nate, and three girls. There were several more of each of the children, a few more recent of Jack and Lulu, and one of two girls in black and white.

Noelle stared at it and realized one of the girls was Lulu when she was a teenager. She recognized Lulu's smile.

She continued through the house and checked out the guest rooms, and one room was dedicated to their granddaughter, decorated with tons of stuffed animals and an overflowing toybox.

As she made her way through the main living space and back toward the kitchen, Noelle admired the pieces of glasswork and pottery tucked into shelves and displayed on tables. She went through a door at the end of the kitchen and found another office space, plus tons of storage and the laundry room.

Next to the desk was another photo of Lulu and the same girl from the black and white photo in the bedroom. It looked like it was taken at the harbor.

Lulu came into the room and collected a bag from the closet. Noelle pointed at the photo. "I love all your old photos. I'm sure this is you, right?"

With a sad look, Lulu said, "Yes and my sister Charlotte. She died a long time ago."

"Oh, I'm so sorry. That's a great photo of the two of you."

Lulu smiled. "It's hard to believe we were ever that young." She took the bag and stepped back into the kitchen.

As Noelle followed, Sam caught her eye. "Let me introduce you to the birthday girl."

Sam put her hand on the shoulder of an attractive blond woman, holding a little girl. The little girl was hiding her face against her mother's shoulder. "Regi, this is Noelle."

Regi smiled. "So glad to meet you. Thank you for coming. I'm so sorry we couldn't see you earlier at the party." She pointed at the little girl. "Emma wasn't feeling well for a few days." She prodded the little girl to say hello, but she refused to budge.

"She's being shy." Regi raised her brows. "Too many people, I think."

"Very nice to meet you," said Noelle. "Happy Birthday. Mine is right before Christmas, so I know what a drag it is to have a birthday at the holidays."

Regi smiled. "So true, but I'm fortunate. These folks always make a big deal of it." She pointed to a tall man standing next to Jack. "That's my husband Nate."

She waved at him, and he hurried over to them and extended his hand. "You must be the Noelle I've heard so much about."

"Uh-oh," said Noelle. She noticed he had the same, almost tropical blue, eyes as his dad. "So nice to meet you, Nate. I've just been admiring your parents' home. It's beautiful."

He nodded. "It fits them. Dad even has a home office up above the garage. It's more than an office. I lived there for a few months when they first moved in here. It's really an apartment."

"I love the view. It's a stunner." She pointed at a framed photo. "I've been admiring all the artwork and photos."

He grinned. "Mom is a collector. She's very involved with the local arts center and theatre."

Jack's deep voice interrupted them and let everyone know the food was ready and to come fill their plates.

The weather was mild enough that she and Carson took

their plates outside and sat on the patio next to the firepit. She pointed toward the sea. "I need to soak up all these water views while I can. I can't believe I leave next week."

He reached for her hand and squeezed it. "You'll be back soon, though."

Izzy and Colin joined them at their outdoor table. "How was your trip to Yakima?" asked Noelle.

Izzy took a sip of wine and sighed. "Long, but it was wonderful to spend time with my parents." She reached for Colin's hand. "I'm really glad to be back home though. I haven't lived here very long like most everyone else, but this is home."

A few minutes later, Sam and Jeff joined them. "This is lovely out here," said Sam.

Izzy turned toward Sam. "Was Linda excited about the cruise?"

Sam grinned. "Oh, yes. Max did well, and she was thrilled. They left early this morning."

As they ate, Noelle savored the view of another sunset over the water. She was certain she would never tire of them. When everyone finished, it was dark and getting chilly. They wandered back inside and a few minutes later, Lulu carried a cake to the dining table and set it in front of Regi.

The group sang the traditional birthday song, and Emma was very interested in helping her mom blow out the candles. When they were extinguished, everyone clapped, and Lulu cut slices of the chocolate cake, while Kate and Sam added scoops of ice cream to them and passed them around to everyone.

The men took their plates and gathered outside, while the ladies stayed at the dining room table. As Izzy finished a bite of her cake, she glanced across the table at Noelle. "Did you have any luck finding any more clues about your birth mother?"

She shook her head. "No. I'm hoping when Bunny is back later this week, she might have a lead from the hospital in Bellingham."

Izzy met Lulu's questioning gaze. "Noelle was left as a newborn at the firehouse here on the island, fifty years ago. She just found out and came here hoping she might track down her birth mother. Do you remember anything about that?"

Lulu tilted her head and looked at Noelle. "I vaguely remember something about that."

Noelle shrugged. "I've been talking to anyone and everyone to see if somebody might remember a pregnancy around that time. There are no birth records that show anyone born here on December twenty-first."

Lulu's face went pale. She wiped her mouth with a napkin and reached for her glass of water. "Excuse me, please. I'm not feeling well."

She made a quick exit toward the master bedroom. Everyone turned from her empty chair and looked at Regi. Izzy frowned. "Has she been sick?"

Regi shook her head. "No. Maybe she ate something that disagreed with her." She took Emma by the hand and asked her to sit in her chair for a minute. "I'll go check on her."

Kate collected the plates. "We should probably go and let Lulu rest. The last thing she needs is a houseful of people if she's not feeling well."

Sam nodded, and they all pitched in and got the kitchen cleaned up. Jack came through the door carrying a stack of empty plates and glanced from the clean table to the clean counters. "Wow, you gals are quick."

Izzy pointed toward the master suite. "Lulu said she

wasn't feeling well. It came on suddenly, so we thought it best to clean up and leave her in peace."

He frowned and put the stack of plates in the sink.

Regi came from the bedroom and shrugged. "She says she's fine, just needs to rest."

Kate came from the patio with the others, and everyone murmured their thanks to Jack and asked that he pass on their best wishes to Lulu.

Carson linked his arm in Noelle's, and they set out for his truck, parked at the very end of the driveway.

As they drove back to town, she turned to him. "Do you know Lulu's maiden name?"

Carson thought for a few seconds and said, "It's Edwards. Her mom was a famous artist. Paintings. Sarah Edwards was her name."

"Oh, interesting. I wonder if some of those paintings in her house are her mom's."

"I'm sure they are. I'm no expert, but I know she was well-known."

He pulled in front of Sam's shop and started to climb from behind the wheel to walk her to her door. She held up her hand and smiled at him. "You don't need to get out. The shop is still open, and I'll be fine."

He frowned at her. "I'll see you tomorrow. We're supposed to be at the winery around five. I'm taking off a little early again and will pick you up about four thirty if that works."

"Sure." She nodded. "I'll be ready. See you then."

She hurried upstairs, anxious to get online and research Lulu and her family. She seemed perfectly fine until Izzy mentioned Noelle was looking for her birth mother. Could Lulu be her?

CHAPTER TWENTY-ONE

After a long night of researching, Noelle slept late the next morning. She threw on some clothes and darted downstairs for a chai tea latte and sat at the kitchen counter to study her notes.

She found a ton of information on Sarah's art, and there was mention of her husband Edward and two daughters Louise and Charlotte, with Charlotte being the youngest.

She finally found an obituary for Charlotte who died when she was in her late twenties. Noelle only learned it was a sudden passing, so she wasn't sure what happened. Charlotte died in Seattle and they had a private service for her.

After an hour of studying, Noelle forced herself to shower and get ready for the day. It was after noon by the time she was dressed, and soup for lunch sounded like a good idea.

She grabbed her handbag and reached for her coat as a knock came from the front door.

Expecting Carson, her eyes widened when Lulu stood before her. "I'm sorry to come over without calling you."

"Don't worry about it. Please, come in."

She opened the door wider and as Lulu stepped inside, she tossed her handbag on the counter.

"Would you like a cup of tea, Lulu?"

She nodded. "That would be lovely."

As she added tea bags to mugs and turned on the kettle, Noelle invited Lulu to sit on the couch. "I hope you're feeling better."

Lulu nodded. "Much better, thank you."

Noelle carried the tea mugs into the living room and gave Lulu one of them before taking her seat at the opposite end of the sofa.

Cradling the cup in her hands, Lulu sighed. "First, I need to apologize. I feel horrible that I ruined the party last night and made everyone leave early."

Noelle shook her head. "No need to apologize. We had a great time but were sorry to see you taken ill."

"It wasn't a physical illness. When you first arrived, there was something about you that seemed familiar to me. Then, when the talk turned to you looking for your birth mother, I got a horrible feeling. I've been visiting my daughter and just came home on Christmas Eve. I didn't know about your story. I talked to Kate and Izzy this morning, and they told me more."

With a sigh, Noelle put her mug on the side table. "I knew something was wrong. I came home last night and tried to find information about your family. Carson told me your mom was a famous artist, and I found lots of information about her work."

In a voice barely above a whisper, Noelle met Lulu's eyes. "Are you my birth mom?"

Tears leaked from Lulu's eyes. She shook her head. "No, I'm not dear. I'm so sorry, but I believe my sister, Charlotte, could be. You have her same gorgeous blue eyes, and she left here when she was just eighteen."

"Was she pregnant?"

"I don't know for sure, but it's possible. Charlotte was the wild child. She gave my parents fits and was constantly sneaking off the island and going to the city. Something happened that summer before you were left at the firehouse. She and my parents had a huge falling out, and she left. I never saw her again. I got a few cards from her for my birthday and holidays over the next ten years, and then my parents received word that they found Charlotte dead in some flophouse in the city."

Noelle gasped. "I'm so sorry. That's awful."

"It was really hard on all of us. I missed her so very much. We'd always been close growing up, only a couple of years apart. When she left like that, so abruptly, I felt so betrayed. I had no idea why she left, and my parents claimed they didn't know."

After a sip of tea, she continued, "Looking back, I think it makes sense that she got pregnant and either she wanted to leave, or my parents made her leave. I don't know for sure. Back then, an unwed mother wasn't something to flaunt. I could see Charlotte bringing the baby back here, thinking someone would take care of her."

Tears leaked onto Lulu's cheeks. Noelle retrieved a box of tissues and set them next to her. "Thank you, dear. I'm so embarrassed and so very sorry. She was in no shape to be a mother or provide a good home or life for you. I know that rings hollow, but I think she thought bringing you back to the island was your best chance."

Noelle reached for a tissue and dried her eyes. "I'd given

up on finding the answers I was so desperate to uncover. I'm in shock. I don't really know what to say."

Lulu smiled at her. "I'm not sure what to say or do either, but I hope you'll be able to find it in your heart to forgive Charlotte someday. I'm not sure what happened to her or why she went down the path she did, but I loved her so much and was devastated when she left and totally bereft when she died."

She blotted her eyes again. "We can do a DNA test to confirm things, but I'm about ninety-nine percent certain you're my niece. I hope you can forgive me, too. I'd love to get to know you and introduce you to Nate's sisters and their families. I know it's not the same as finding your mother, but I would be so grateful if you would consider letting me be part of your life, Noelle."

Noelle bit her lip as tears streamed down her face. "You have nothing to be forgiven for, Lulu. You've given me the answers I've been hoping for. I'd love to know the whole story, but like you said, nobody knows exactly what happened. With your parents and Charlotte gone, we'll never know."

"I'm sure she thought someone on the island would adopt you. Maybe she even hoped my parents would, I don't know. Izzy told me wonderful parents adopted you." She smiled. "I'm so very glad they gave you a happy life."

"The happiest." Noelle's voice cracked. "I miss them very much. I lost my mom earlier this year."

With a tiny nod of her head, Lulu reached out for Noelle's hand. "I know how hard that is. I was a mess when my mom passed. I know I'm not who you were searching for, but if you'll have me, I'll do my darndest to be the best aunt you can imagine."

Noelle moved closer to Lulu and embraced her. Through

tears, she whispered, "I would like nothing more than to be your niece and get to know you better."

Once they dried their faces and composed themselves, Noelle asked Lulu to join her for lunch at Soup D'Jour. After lunch, Lulu took Noelle to her doctor's office, and they submitted samples for a DNA test.

They spent the afternoon sitting in Sam's coffee shop, sipping lattes while Noelle told Lulu all about her childhood and her life. She showed her photos of Courtney, and Lulu shared photos of her daughters and their children.

When Noelle looked up and saw it was almost time for Carson to pick her up, she panicked. "Are you and Jack going to the winery tonight?"

Lulu grinned. "Wouldn't miss it. Wine is one of my favorite things."

"Are you okay with me telling the others you're my aunt and the story of your sister?"

With a sad look in her eyes, Lulu nodded. "Of course. I'm delighted to shout it from the rooftops that I've found my long-lost niece. I couldn't be happier. I'm only sad that it took so long and that my sister made such horrible choices that impacted a sweet baby girl."

"Like I said, none of this is anything you need to be sorry for. I'm just thrilled I have my answer. I couldn't have asked for a better family to be a part of. I never even thought about the idea of an extended family. I was so focused on my birth mom. I wish I could have met her, but my mom always said things work out like they're supposed to. I think she was right."

Lulu squeezed her hand. "I think your mom was wise. I tend to believe that, too. I only wish I could have met her."

Noelle hugged her goodbye and promised to see her at the winery. She hurried upstairs to change clothes and had just slipped her earrings in when Carson arrived. He took one look at her and tilted his head. "What's up? You look like Justice when she removes a squeaker from her toys."

She gripped his arm as they descended the stairs. "I found my birth mom."

His eyes went wide. "That's terrific. Who is she?"

On the way to the winery, she explained her research and Lulu's surprise visit. "We're going to tell the others tonight."

He pulled into the parking lot, and, once he opened her door for her, he enveloped her in a long and tight hug. "I'm so glad you found your family, Noelle. You couldn't find a better person than Lulu. I never knew her sister, but Lulu is a true gem."

With his arm around her, they walked to the entrance where they found Blake and Ellie. Noelle could barely contain her excitement but was determined to wait until everyone, including Lulu, arrived so they could tell their friends the good news.

As she sipped the delicious wine and nibbled on cheese, her mind drifted to the future. Spending time with Lulu only intensified her desire to move to the island. Not only would she be gaining a community of friends, but she'd have a real family.

If she got the job, it would be the icing on the cake, but regardless, she would make Friday Harbor her home. With that decision firm in her mind, Noelle had to tell Courtney the whole story and let her know she would be selling the house.

That was a problem for tomorrow. For tonight, she would savor the happiness in her heart surrounded by the friends she adored, the man she was falling in love with, and the aunt she never dreamed of knowing.

As the others arrived, Lulu made a beeline for Noelle and

slipped her arm into hers. Lulu glanced over at Noelle and picked up a spoon to hit against her glass. "Are you ready?"

Noelle smiled at her. "So ready."

A few minutes before midnight on the last day of the year, Noelle stood at the railing of the harbor with Carson's arm wrapped around her. They'd eaten, visited. and danced for hours at the New Year's Eve party. Now, they were poised to take in the fireworks that would bid farewell to the past and ring in the future.

What a bright future it was destined to be.

After her initial shock at the revelation of Noelle's abandonment and search for her birth mother, topped off with the news that she was planning to relocate, Courtney took it in stride, told her mother she was happy for her, and promised to visit as soon as she could make it work.

Noelle had spent the last few days at Lulu's house, immersed in the family history and learning all about Lulu's life and her family. They even had a video chat with her daughters so Lulu could introduce the cousins to each other.

The last few days had been surreal. Noelle never imagined finding such happiness when she set out for the island three weeks ago.

The crowd was counting down, and, when the clock struck midnight, Carson bent and kissed her. His gentle touch marked a new beginning. One that Noelle couldn't wait to embrace.

As the colorful fireworks exploded and lit up the sky, it was as if all of Noelle's dreams burst to life. In Lulu, she'd found the steadiness and wisdom she'd longed for since losing her mom. In Carson, she'd stumbled upon a stable and loving man, one who she could imagine spending the rest of her life with, and in the others, she'd discovered a community of true and trusted friends.

She held Carson's hand as the fireworks continued to light up the inky sky. She couldn't imagine life getting much better than this. Not only had she found her roots but a future filled with excitement and hope.

With her hand firmly entwined in Carson's, Noelle was sure this would be the best year of her life.

EPILOGUE

As the harbor came into view out of the large window where Noelle sat at her table, she grabbed her handbag and started downstairs to the car deck. It wouldn't be long before the ferry arrived in Friday Harbor, and she was anxious to see Carson and everyone else.

It had taken everything in her to keep the secret she had. Carson had come to visit over President's Day, and they'd had fun exploring Walla Walla. She hadn't seen him since, having completed her interview with the mayor and his staff over a video call.

Now, with the offer and her acceptance of the position, she couldn't wait to tell him she'd be moving to Friday Harbor in June. She found the thought of packing and moving overwhelming but tried to concentrate on the prize. She'd be living on the island she'd come to love, close to Aunt Lulu and the family of cousins she never imagined.

Not to mention, she and Carson could spend more time together and explore their budding relationship.

Even Courtney was excited. She and Phil planned a trip

to visit later in the summer before they went back for their final year of college. Thankfully, they'd decided to marry after they graduated, so she wouldn't have to help with a wedding until next summer.

That would give her time to get organized in the new house Jack promised he'd find her. Lulu wanted her to stay with them until she found a house. Lulu had already served Jack his eviction notice from the apartment. Noelle had sworn her and Jack to secrecy and wanted to share the good news with Carson and everyone else in person.

She had ten glorious days of spring break to spend in the San Juan Islands. She and Carson had plans to visit Orcas Island, and he wanted to take her fishing. They also had an appointment at the breeder's to check out the puppies. Jack was ready to take her and Carson on tours of homes and neighborhoods where she might want to live. He was also coordinating the sale of her house in Walla Walla.

A small home like Betty's sounded perfect to Noelle. She was ready to downsize and didn't want the work of a large piece of property or a huge house to maintain.

As Noelle thought about her parents, and especially her mom, who had kept her secret for fifty years, but obviously wanted Noelle to know and even find her lost family, a tear slipped from her eye. Her mom would be pleased to know she had a loving aunt and uncle, not to mention cousins galore. Noelle's only regret was that her mother never got to meet them.

Along with the excitement of a new beginning, a bit of apprehension niggled at the back of her mind. She'd been in the same house and same town for decades. All her memories of Tom were there. It was bittersweet. She knew he would want her to be happy. To take a chance. He was always more of a risk-taker than she was.

As they pulled into the landing, a beam of sunlight reflected off the ring she wore on her right hand and made her squint. It was a ring Tom had given her for their first anniversary. The sparkles from the sun hitting the diamonds circling the eternity ring made her smile. She drove off the apron and onto Front Street, confident that Tom had sent her a message.

She set out for Lulu's house, where she would be staying during her visit. She had time to drop her things and then head to Sam's, where everyone was gathering for a welcome back dinner in honor of Noelle.

Her heart was full and for the first time in a very long time, she was excited about the future and the possibilities that awaited her on the island. To think all of what awaited her now was due to that tiny leap of faith she took to come home for Christmas.

There was mention of Lavender Valley, Oregon, in this book. Lavender Valley is the setting for Tammy's new *Sisters of the Heart Series*, where Georgia and her foster sisters each get their own story. Read the prequel, GREETINGS FROM LAVENDER VALLEY, to learn more about all the women featured in this six-book series.

If you're new to the Hometown Harbor Series, you'll want to read the other books, each featuring a different heroine, starting with FINDING HOME, Sam's story. If you haven't yet discovered the Glass Beach Cottage Trilogy, you'll want to start with BEACH HAVEN, where you'll meet Lily, who is grieving and looking for a bit of hope and happiness in a new coastal community. For those who enjoy whodunits, check out the Cooper Harrington Detective

Novels, with KILLER MUSIC being the first book in the series.

If you've missed reading any of this series, here are the links to the other books. All but the free prequel are available in print and eBook formats.

Prequel: Hometown Harbor: The Beginning (free prequel novella eBook only)
Book 1: Finding Home
Book 2: Home Blooms
Book 3: A Promise of Home
Book 4: Pieces of Home
Book 5: Finally Home
Book 6: Forever Home
Book 7: Follow Me Home
Book 8: Long Way Home

ACKNOWLEDGMENTS

I love Christmas, and I love escaping to the San Juan Islands with my characters in this series. When this idea came to me one morning, I couldn't let it go and sat down to write this new Christmas story as a treat for my loyal readers who enjoy this series. It's a little shorter than my other stories, but I poured all the feels of the season into this one.

If you haven't yet read my *Sisters of the Heart Series*, I hope you'll be inspired to try it after meeting Georgia in this book. She is a wonderful character and gets her own story in the series set in Lavender Valley.

Many thanks to my editor, Susan, for finding my mistakes and helping me polish *Come Home for Christmas.* She does an awesome job, and I'm grateful for her. All the credit for this gorgeous cover goes to Elizabeth Mackey, who never disappoints. I'm fortunate to have such an incredible team helping me.

My dad was a volunteer fireman and chief in our small town for decades. He never found a baby at their fire station, but I couldn't resist this story that tugged at me for several days. Although Noelle was left long before the laws came into play about safe places to leave babies, firemen are always there to help, especially those who need it most. I also had fun with

Sheriff Mercer. A loyal reader wrote and suggested I use a firefighter or police officer in one of my stories. With my dad being both, it was a no-brainer, so I hope she enjoys this special story.

I so appreciate all of the readers who have taken the time to tell their friends about my work and provide reviews of my books. These reviews are especially important in promoting future books, so if you enjoy my novels, please consider leaving a review. I also encourage you to follow me on Amazon, Goodreads, and BookBub, where leaving a review is even easier, and you'll be the first to know about new releases and deals.

Remember to visit my website at http://www.tammylgrace.com and join my mailing list for my exclusive group of readers. I also have a fun Book Buddies Facebook Group. That's the best place to find me and get a chance to participate in my giveaways. Join my Facebook group at https://www.facebook.com/groups/AuthorTammyLGraceBookBuddies/
and keep in touch—I'd love to hear from you.

Happy Reading,

Tammy

MORE BY TAMMY L. GRACE

COOPER HARRINGTON DETECTIVE NOVELS

Killer Music

Deadly Connection

Dead Wrong

Cold Killer

Deadly Deception

HOMETOWN HARBOR SERIES

Hometown Harbor: The Beginning (Prequel Novella)

Finding Home

Home Blooms

A Promise of Home

Pieces of Home

Finally Home

Forever Home

Follow Me Home

Long Way Home

CHRISTMAS STORIES

A Season for Hope: Christmas in Silver Falls Book 1

The Magic of the Season: Christmas in Silver Falls Book 2

Christmas in Snow Valley: A Hometown Christmas Book 1

One Unforgettable Christmas: A Hometown Christmas Book 2

Christmas Wishes: Souls Sisters at Cedar Mountain Lodge

Christmas Surprises: Soul Sisters at Cedar Mountain Lodge

GLASS BEACH COTTAGE SERIES

Beach Haven

Moonlight Beach

Beach Dreams

WRITING AS CASEY WILSON

A Dog's Hope

A Dog's Chance

WISHING TREE SERIES

The Wishing Tree

Wish Again

Overdue Wishes

One More Wish

SISTERS OF THE HEART SERIES

Greetings from Lavender Valley

Pathway to Lavender Valley

Sanctuary at Lavender Valley

Blossoms at Lavender Valley

Comfort in Lavender Valley

Reunion in Lavender Valley

FROM THE AUTHOR

Thank you for reading the ninth book in the Hometown Harbor Series. If you enjoyed it and are a fan of women's fiction, you'll want to try my GLASS BEACH COTTAGE SERIES, set in Driftwood Bay, or my newest series, SISTERS OF THE HEART. You can even start this one by downloading the first book, GREETINGS FROM LAVENDER VALLEY, for FREE!

The two books I've written as Casey Wilson, A DOG'S HOPE and A DOG'S CHANCE, both have received enthusiastic support from my readers and, if you're a dog lover, are must reads.

If you enjoy holiday stories, be sure to check out my CHRISTMAS IN SILVER FALLS SERIES and HOMETOWN CHRISTMAS SERIES. They are small-town Christmas stories of hope, friendship, and family. I'm also one of the authors of the bestselling SOUL SISTERS AT CEDAR MOUNTAIN LODGE SERIES, centered around a woman who opens her heart and home to four foster girls one Christmas.

If mysteries are among your favorite genres, be sure to explore my COOPER HARRINGTON DETECTIVE NOVELS. Readers love the characters, including a loyal golden retriever and the plot twists that keep them guessing until the end.

I'm also one of the founding authors of *My Book Friends* and invite you to join this fun group of readers and authors on Facebook. I'd love to send you my exclusive interview with the canine companions in my *Hometown Harbor Series* as a thank you for joining my exclusive group of readers. You can sign up by following at my website here: https://www.tammylgrace.com/newsletter

I hope you'll connect with me on social media. You can find me on Facebook, where I have a page and a special group for my readers and follow me on Amazon and BookBub, so you'll know when I have a new release or a deal. If you haven't yet, be sure to download the free novella, HOMETOWN HARBOR: THE BEGINNING. It's a prequel to FINDING HOME that I know you'll enjoy.

If you did enjoy this book or any of my other books, I'd be grateful if you took a few minutes to leave a short review on Amazon, BookBub, Goodreads, or any of the other retailers you use.

ABOUT THE AUTHOR

Tammy L. Grace is the *USA Today* bestselling and award-winning author of the Cooper Harrington Detective Novels, the bestselling Hometown Harbor Series, and the Glass Beach Cottage Series, along with several sweet Christmas novellas. Tammy also writes under the pen name of Casey Wilson for Bookouture and Grand Central. You'll find Tammy online at www.tammylgrace.com where you can join her mailing list and be part of her exclusive group of readers. Connect with Tammy on Facebook at www.facebook.com/tammylgrace.books or Instagram at @authortammylgrace.

- f facebook.com/tammylgrace.books
- 🐦 twitter.com/TammyLGrace
- 📷 instagram.com/authortammylgrace
- BB bookbub.com/authors/tammy-l-grace
- g goodreads.com/tammylgrace
- a amazon.com/author/tammylgrace

Made in United States
Orlando, FL
03 October 2024